Michael, wait for me

Other books by Patricia Calvert

Bigger
Sooner
Glennis, Before and After

Michael, wait for me

PATRICIA CALVERT

ATHENEUM BOOKS FOR YOUNG READERS
NEW YORK • LONDON • TORONTO • SYDNEY • SINGAPORE

In loving memory of Helen Patricia Frank—
mother, mentor, friend

Atheneum Books for Young Readers
An imprint of Simon & Schuster Children's Publishing Division
1230 Avenue of the Americas
New York, New York 10020

Book design by Ann Bobco

The text of this book is set in Granjon.

Printed in the United States of America

10 9 8 7 6 5 4 3 2 1
Library of Congress Cataloging-in-Publication Data
Calvert, Patricia.
Michael, wait for me / by Patricia Calvert.
p. cm.
Summary: Sixth-grader Sarah develops a crush on the troubled young man
that her older sister brings home from college for the summer.
ISBN 0-689-82102-6
[1. Sisters—Fiction. 2. Interpersonal relations—Fiction. 3. Emotional problems—Fiction.
4. Suicide—Fiction.] I. Title.
PZ7.C139Mi 2000 [Fic]—dc21 99-19104

FIRST
EDITION

chapter one

"I thought we'd put him in your room," my mother explained matter-of-factly. "It'll be more convenient for everyone that way."

I stared at her. She made the announcement as if it were a perfect solution. I watched steam rise from the spaghetti sauce she was making. It made her hair limp and glued it to her temples in wet little curls, the kind you see on sweaty babies.

I couldn't believe she meant what she said.

"Excuse me?" I yelled. "Why in *my* room?" School had only been out for a week. This definitely wasn't news I was glad to get. My mother quit stirring the pot of sauce and looked at me. She shaped her lips in a round *O* of amazement. That's because basically I'm not the kind of person who ever does much yelling.

"Convenient? For who?" I said a little louder. "Not for yours truly, that's for sure!" Once I got the hang of it, raising my voice felt sort of good. Empowering, my English teacher, Mrs. Graham, would've said.

I leaned forward and gave my head a smack against the tabletop. My reaction might upset my mother so much she'd drop her spoon and rush to my side. She'd hug me, tell me it was just a joke, that of course she was only kidding.

She didn't budge.

"How come you can't stick this turkey in Joey's room?" I demanded. I'd hit my head too hard. I could feel a little lump begin to rise right in the middle of my forehead.

"I'll go down to the laundry room this minute and get the rollaway out. If you'll help me haul it upstairs we can put it in Joey's—"

"Now, Sarah," my mother murmured, and resumed stirring her sauce. "Now, Sarah. You know perfectly well your brother's room is hardly more than a large closet. Joey helped me move the cot into Kimberlee's room while you were outside helping Dad. You can bunk with her."

Then she pointed out, ever so reasonably, "If this young man is going to be here all summer, I want him to be comfortable."

I hate it when my mother is reasonable. When she talks to me as if she's dealing with a crabby three-year-old.

"And I wish you wouldn't call this fellow a turkey, Sarah," she added, almost as an afterthought. "He's not a turkey, dear. His name is Michael Miller, and I want you to treat him as nicely as you'd treat anyone who came to Brookfield for a visit. Kim says he comes from a very fine family. His father's a doctor, the kind who operates on people's hearts."

I explored the tender spot on my forehead with the tip of my finger. I didn't exactly like the way she said *he comes from a very fine family,* as if somehow ours didn't amount to much. Would we have to spend the entire summer pretending to be people we weren't, just so dear Kimmy could make a big impression on this new guy she was hauling home from St. Alban's?

And that part about treating him as nicely as I'd treat anyone who showed up for a visit. Well, nobody'd ever come to hog the whole summer before.

I rubbed my forehead and made a silent vow. I'd cut my wrists before I let Michael Miller think I gave up my room voluntarily. I wouldn't waste a minute letting him know it was taken away from me without due legal process. As if I were someone who didn't have any civil rights, like people you see on TV who come to work in America but don't have green cards yet.

Ergo—it's a Latin word that means "therefore," in case you didn't know—I intended to give this turkey such a cold shoulder he'd think he was spending the summer in Siberia. Not to mention I'd think up some kind of exquisite torture for my sister, Kim, who actually was the person responsible for the whole mess in the first place.

After all, it was my summer too. A fact certain people didn't seem to understand. No way did I intend to give it up to a total stranger without a darn good fight.

chapter two

Because for one thing—surprise, surprise—I'd been thinking about having company of my own for a change.

Not that I'm the social type, for sure not like my sister, Kimberlee, who got a Miss Congeniality award when she was in eleventh grade. But the idea of having company occurred to me after I caught Jason Conrad looking at me funny in sixth-grade science class just before school let out for the summer. I mentioned Jason's look— astonished, as if he'd never seen me before—to my best friend, Katie Albright.

"Hey, babe, he's got the hots for you," she told me as we cleaned out our lockers on the last day of school. She rolled her eyes like it could be the beginning of the romance of the century. Please.

"Yeah, right," I said. "Never in this earthly life will Jason Conrad know hot from cold." Not to mention Jason usually was even quieter than I was.

But once I found out he might like me a little I began to think how neat it'd be if sometimes he could come out and help me clean kennels. Or how maybe he could pick up a video before he rode his bike out from town and we could watch it on the TV we keep on the front porch while my folks watched in the family room. Which—considering Jason and I were both quiet types—would save us having to make too much conversation. Plus, I wanted to have Katie or Camilla (my second best friend) out for overnights once in a while, just like I did other summers.

But all that was B. M., Before Michael.

"I don't see why this guy has to stay so long," I complained to my mother as I massaged the lump on my forehead. By hook or crook, I intended to restake a claim to my own room.

"Just consider, Mom. It means any plans Joey or I had for the summer will go down the tube. Every bed in the house will be taken. Including the rollaway. Neither me nor Joey can have a single person sleep over for three whole months. Any good lawyer would call that cruel and unusual punishment, which must be against the Constitution. Joey or I can't have a social life till those idiot lovebirds go back to college in September."

My sister said what was going on between her and this latest boyfriend was more than an ordinary infatuation. She'd already had enough of those to fill a book. Kim told my folks in a letter that she and Michael were thinking about getting married after they graduated.

Of course, I wasn't supposed to know anything about that. I'd overheard Mom and Dad talking about it in the kitchen one day when they didn't realize I could hear every word they said because I was right outside under the open window, washing the dogs' food pans.

When my mother turned to face me again, her flushed cheeks matched the pink stripes in her shirt. She brushed one of her wet curls away with the back of her hand. "Now, Sarah," she sighed, still hopelessly reasonable. "Now, Sarah."

Someday, I'm going to sit my parents down and give them the third degree about that name. "Why did you guys stick me with Sarah after you gave my sister a killer name like Kimberlee, with two *e*'s?"

I hope they can come up with a good explanation. When I was younger—like back in third or fourth grade—it didn't matter much, but lately it'd started to really stress me out. Had they picked Kimberlee for her because she looked like a cover girl model the minute she was born? Did I get Sarah because I looked like a librarian?

Six months ago I told my mother I wanted to have it changed. That was even before I knew Jason Conrad might like me. If there were legal costs I told her I'd pay for them out of my allowance. I was thinking of Darla or Raquel or Natalee. Something with a little flair. And maybe two *e*'s.

"Sarah is a lovely name," my mother insisted patiently. "Some wonderful women have been named Sarah."

"Name two," I challenged.

"Sarah Bernhardt, for instance," she said. "She was a fine actress, and people still say nice things about her. Sarah Williams, for another."

"Sarah Bernhardt's dead, Mom." I knew that because once I'd seen a documentary about famous dead people. "Everyone says nice things about a person when they're gone. And who, pray tell, is Sarah Williams?"

"I went to college with her. She majored in chemistry and now is the research director for a famous cosmetics company in Paris."

"See? Bernhardt's dead and Williams was forced to leave the land of her birth because she had a bad case of plain-name syndrome."

"Now, Sarah," my mother said with another long sigh. "Now, Sarah."

If I ever get hit by a car and lie near death in a hospital in a distant city, my family probably will gather around me to pay their final respects. My mother will lean over me and whisper softly, *Now, Sarah; now, Sarah,* as if that's all it'll take to talk me out of dying.

I whisked the red and white checked cloth off the table and draped it over my shoulders like a cape. "I just don't see why Kimmy has to keep dragging guys home all the time," I whined piteously.

"Goodness, you certainly sound whiny today," my mother observed correctly.

At Christmas, the first year Kim went off to college, it was the captain of the football team. He didn't have a neck, only a pair of humongous shoulders that started right under his earlobes and made it impossible for him to get through doorways unless he turned sideways.

He did pushups in front of the TV every afternoon and drank Gatorade by the gallon. My brother, Joey, was crazy about him. His name was Brad or Chad or Tad or something. He talked football to my dad, a man who's never watched a game all the way through in his life.

He didn't understand that my dad's life was dogs. As far back as I can remember he's joked about that. "After I got married, my life just went to the dogs," Dad likes to say, winking at Mom and smiling in that lopsided way I like.

If you didn't know my dad was just about the best professional show dog trainer in the country, that the Brookfield Boarding and Training Kennel was famous as far away as Connecticut to the east and California to the west, you'd think for sure Dan Connelly's life had been a serious disappointment to him.

"Sarah, put that tablecloth back where it belongs," my mother said. I left it where it was, huddling under it as if I were chilled to the bone. I watched her chop garlic, onion, and fresh oregano on a plastic cutting board at the counter.

Have you ever noticed how everyone's mother has a certain way of doing what she does? Katie's flaps around their kitchen as if it belongs to a stranger and she's still trying to figure out where the sugar and flour are. Camilla Johnson's floats around hers like she's got other things on her mind. Actually, she does. She and Mr. J. are getting a divorce and Camilla thinks she and her brother and her mom will have to move into an apartment, which means she might not be able to keep her cat, Abigail. My mother works efficiently, like you hope nurses do if they're taking care of you after emergency surgery.

It started to get hot under the tablecloth, but I folded up the edge of it to make a hood for my cape. I began to get a little sweaty. With luck I might start to look feverish. My mother would think I was coming down with something. The turkey Kimmy was dragging home for the summer would have to be sent away. Or he might take one look at me—cranky and flushed and feverish—and decide to leave without being asked. Presto! The summer would be mine again.

Without actually glancing in my direction, my mother guessed what I was up to. "Now, Sarah, I told you to put that cloth back on the table," she said firmly. "You're making yourself look sick. Besides, it's not hygienic for people to put tablecloths on their heads."

So much for inspiring her sense of motherly concern.

I shook out the cloth, smoothed it across the table, then dragged myself upstairs.

"Why don't you start moving things out of your room?" my mother called after me. "That way, Michael can get himself settled as soon as he and Kimmy arrive this afternoon."

Sure enough, the rollaway was all made up and shoved into the darkest corner of Kim's room. I started to haul stuff out my room across the hall—boom box, junk from the floor of my closet, a ton of stuffed bears, which I'd collected for ages. I tried to use as many hangers as possible in my sister's closet, which amounted to only three because I don't wear many clothes that need hangers.

I heaved myself onto the rollaway. It was lumpy and sagged in the middle. I got up and threw myself into the middle of Kim's bed. If she didn't like it, too bad.

I stared at the walls. Her room was painted peach, the color of her hair. Her hair's curly too, like Mom's. Mine's the color of burlap and can't spell a four-letter word like "curl." I sniffed. Even though Kim hadn't been home since Easter everything still smelled good, just like she always did.

I cried.

I knew nobody loved me.

I felt like an orphan.

I've noticed it sometimes makes a person feel sort of happy to think they're an orphan that nobody cares about. That fairy tale, "The Little Match Girl," was one of my favorites when I was little.

I was enjoying orphanhood and feeling totally unloved when I heard a car door slam outside. Next, I heard Kim laugh. As usual, my sister sounded happy and upbeat. I chewed my knuckles and groaned.

"They're here," my mother called up the stairs. She sounded upbeat too. I definitely wasn't, so I lay there and nibbled my knuckles as if they were Mars bars.

"Sarah, did you hear me?" my mother called again. This time there was an edge of annoyance in her voice. "They're here."

"So? They're going to be here all summer," I yelled back. "Eventually I'm sure we'll all get acquainted on our way to or from the bathroom."

Three months. It might as well be three years. Once, I read an article in *Scholastic* about cryogenics. That's where they freeze you after you sign a paper to let people know when you want to be thawed out. Maybe I could get myself frozen till September and be thawed out a couple days before school started. Why not? For sure the summer was worthless to me now.

The dogs in the kennels out back, stirred up by the sound of slamming doors and unfamiliar voices, began to raise a ruckus. Three days ago someone from Kansas had shipped Dad a Labrador retriever named Bingo, and I could hear his mellow boom above the others.

Bingo's only a nickname. His registered name is a mouthful—St. John's Lord of the Waters. The St. John's part refers to how Labradors probably originated during the 1600s on St. John's Island, off the east coast of Canada. They started out as a fisherman's dog, helping to pull nets up onto the beaches, then later were crossbred with English hunting dogs. Now they're just about the most popular breed of retriever in the country.

At first, his owners, Colonel and Mrs. Wortham, worried Bingo might get too tall and too heavy to be eligible for competition, but he's holding steady at twenty-four inches at the shoulder and tips the scale at a hair under seventy-five pounds. He's the color of a night with no moon or stars, except for a single white teardrop in the middle of his chest. He's so good-natured you wouldn't believe it. Of course, he's strictly a kennel dog, but he'd love to cuddle with you. It'd be like trying to hold an elephant on your lap, though.

I quit chewing my knuckles. Thinking about Bingo suddenly gave me a glimmer of hope. Because, would you believe it, that hunky-lunky football captain Kimmy dragged home for Christmas turned out to have a weird phobia about dogs. He said his mother told him he'd been frightened by a neighbor's poodle when he was only two years old and it'd left a scar deep in his subconscious. He decided to leave Brookfield before New Year's.

Hey. Maybe this new guy had a subconscious and a phobia to go with it. I imagined what might happen: Kim would take Michael Miller out to the kennels, he'd take one look at the dozens of pooches we've got back there, and he'd have some kind of panic attack. He'd turn pale. His knees would quiver like Jell-O. He'd ask to leave after only a couple days.

Please, Lord, give Michael Miller a phobia, I prayed. To be on the safe side, why not give him two?

The possibility my prayer might be answered cheered me up so much that when Mom called about supper being ready in twenty minutes I got up and went to the top of the stairs. I heard my folks and Kim and Joey nattering away in the kitchen in those high, fakey voices people use when they suddenly discover there's a stranger in their midst.

I leaned over the bannister. Just then, el boyfriendo stepped out of the kitchen into the front hall on his way to get another load of luggage from the car. He hesitated a moment. I noticed one thing right away: This one had a neck. He was tall and thin and wouldn't have to turn sideways to get through any doorway. I squinted down at him, hoping to detect signs of a phobia.

Behind him, the light came through the little round window in the hall and shone on his hair, which hung just below his ears. It was such a pale color it seemed almost white, and the sun polished it till it gleamed like the helmet of a medieval knight. I had the feeling he was a person nobody ever called Mike. Not Mickey either. He was strictly a Michael.

He glanced up the stairs. He didn't seem surprised or embarrassed to see me looking down at him. He didn't smile, just sort of turned up the corners of his mouth in a quirky way. His eyebrows were dark, and when he raised them as if he were about to ask me a question, they looked like a bird's wings. Beneath them, his eyes were as blue as the colored bottle my mother fills with yellow strawflowers and keeps on the windowsill above the kitchen sink.

I didn't smile either.

"You must be Sarah," he said in a mild, thoughtful voice.

You must be Sarah.

As if Kim had already told him lots of stuff about me. As if he'd actually paid attention to what she said. Like maybe he was even a little bit curious about the kind of person I'd turn out to be.

I touched the lump in the middle of my forehead. I hoped it didn't look too much like a zit. Something happened under my ribs. My heart slipped out of its usual place and got wedged accidentally between my lungs or liver or spleen or whatever's there inside your chest. Jason Conrad may've gotten an A in health science, but my knowledge of human anatomy was still a little fuzzy.

Whether I'd given my room up voluntarily or not,

I knew when I looked down at Michael Miller and he looked up at me that the summer was going to be more different than I'd imagined. What I never guessed was how the whole family would be changed by the time September came. Including Bingo.

chapter three

The next morning I got up early. Kim was still asleep, curled on her side like a comma, her peachy hair spread in waves across her pillow. She was snoring a little. Nothing gross, just soft little wuffles that sounded kind of sweet. I tiptoed past her bed. It's not easy to hate a person who looks as innocent as a puppy when she's sleeping.

I grabbed a pair of shorts and a clean tank top out of the cardboard box where I'd stuffed them yesterday. Kim didn't stir as I sneaked down the hall to the bathroom. I glanced at the door of my room. It was closed. No doubt His Royal Mightiness was sleeping soundly in my bed. I wondered if he'd noticed the water stains on my ceiling yet, or how one of them looked exactly like the head of a wild horse.

I washed my face and raked my wet fingers through my hair. It was a perfect morning to take the boat out. Three summers ago, when Dad first got it— a used one he'd picked up cheap—it was so popular with the whole family that we had to take numbers to use it. Now, except for the times I took it out myself, the boat stayed tied up at the dock where it rocked gently all day long, growing scum on its bottom.

It was a quiet morning, but I figured I could set the jib just enough to catch a puff of air that'd take me out to the middle of the lake. Once I got out there, I'd lie down in the bottom of the boat and stay till I was good and ready to come ashore. Which might be a while, so when I passed through the kitchen I made a peanut butter sandwich, grabbed the latest issue of *Show Dog Journal* off the counter, and eased out the back door without a sound.

Five A.M. is a great time in Wisconsin in the summer. In our neighborhood, everyone owns about ten acres of land, giving all of us plenty of privacy. Hardly anyone gets up at five, so I knew I wouldn't hear a sound until at least eight o'clock when Mr. Gregory down the road set off to scour the countryside for antiques, which he resold for big bucks at his shop, Aunt Annie's Attic.

Sheets of fog covered the surface of the water. The sun, not quite up yet, tinted the layers shades of dove gray and mouse-ear pink. And since bare feet on wet morning grass don't make any sound, I saw el boyfriendo before he saw me.

"Give me a break already!" I muttered under my breath. That closed door across the hall didn't mean a darned thing. There he was on the dock, the thief who'd hijacked my summer. He was staring thoughtfully down at the boat as if he intended to climb into it himself.

Fine. Let him. I stopped in midstride, sure he hadn't seen me yet. I'd just go back to the house and forget about—

But he turned before I could get my feet moving in the opposite direction. He raised his hand in a polite little wave. "Hi, Sarah," he said in the kind of hushed voice people use in museums.

I nodded. I didn't intend to talk to him and I sure didn't intend to be friendly. That's how I was at supper last night too. I watched him eat two helpings of spaghetti, which my mother made so often you'd think we were Italian instead of Irish. His appetite was guaranteed to make her love him forever, which made me feel even more spiteful than before.

El boyfriendo may have had two helpings of spaghetti, but I hardly ate a thing myself because my stomach was tied up in knots. It was bad enough that he loved my mother's cooking and was going to camp in my room for the whole summer, but the way he looked at Kimmy made me want to vomit comets. To say his eyes were filled with love sounds corny, but it was disgustingly true.

Then I noticed something even worse. Michael Miller studied my parents with surprised glances that also were suspiciously tender.

What? He'd only been at Brookfield for a couple hours, so what gave him the right? They were *our* parents, Kim's and Joey's and mine. He had a pair of his own, didn't he? If he had any tender glances to spare why didn't he fax them home where they belonged?

Michael pointed a bare toe at the name painted in green letters on the transom. "I'll bet that was your idea," he said.

"What makes you so smart?" I snapped.

"Kimberlee told me you're a big King Arthur buff. The *Guinevere*. Guess I didn't have to be a rocket scientist to figure out you were responsible." He cocked his head and gave me a curious look. "Do you know what that name means?"

I gave him a frosty stare.

"Guinevere was the daughter of Prince Leodegran. In Welsh, her name means 'white phantom,' and originally it was spelled Gwenhwyfar." He smiled one of his quirky smiles. "You couldn't have picked a better name for a white sailboat."

What he said was sort of intriguing, but I pretended it wasn't. "Um. It's one thing for *me* to be interested in those old tales," he went on. "I mean, I'm majoring in medieval literature. But it seems a little unusual for a girl your age to be into stuff like that."

I snorted. "What do you know about girls my age?" I was supposed to believe he combined research about medieval times with field studies of female sixth graders? "Anyway, my King Arthur phase was a million years ago. I'm over it now," I said. Which was true. I hadn't thought about Guinevere or King Arthur or Merlin or anything that happened in those long-ago, make-believe times since I decided for sure I wanted to be a professional dog handler.

We stood side by side, staring at the boat. Dragged up on the beach nearby was the old rowboat we used to use, turned upside down so it wouldn't collect water. "Do you want to take her out before everyone else gets up?" Michael asked, ignoring the fact I was giving him my best "Welcome to Siberia" treatment. It was obvious he didn't have the rowboat in mind.

Not with you, I wanted to tell him. "Go ahead if you want," I muttered. "I only came down to make sure Joey tied her up last night." Talk about a bald-faced lie. I knew perfectly well the *Guinevere* was tied up properly because I'd checked on her just before I went to bed.

Michael hesitated. "Well, maybe I will," he said. He stepped gingerly off the dock and down into the boat. I could tell right away he didn't have a clue about what to do next, that he didn't know diddly about lowering a centerboard or raising a sail or handling a rudder.

"How much sailing have you done?" I asked in the tone of voice Mrs. Graham uses when somebody's late with their English assignments.

He looked up at me with a sheepish expression in his bottle-blue eyes. "Not much, to be honest." He grinned slightly. "None, to be even honester."

"I don't think there's such a word as 'honester'," I said. "Echo Lake's deep in the middle, and cold too. Dad says he thinks it's fed by an old glacier spring left over from the ice age." I looked at him like I did at Joey when he'd done something really dumb.

"What if you accidentally drowned out there? Your folks might sue us. We could lose Brookfield Kennels. Kim wouldn't be able to finish college. Our lives would be ruined."

I was pleased when the grim scenario I painted caused a stricken expression to cross Michael Miller's face, making his eyes suddenly less blue. I untied the *Guinevere,* hopped into it myself, then gave a hard shove off the dock.

"Here—" I threw a life jacket at him. "State law says you've got to wear one of these." Before he could ask, "Where's yours?" I grabbed a vest off the floor of the boat and slung it over one arm while I lowered the centerboard and raised the mainsail. Michael closed the Velcro fasteners on his vest, then sat down as timidly as a little kid on the first day of preschool.

I tacked away from the dock. Once we got a couple hundred feet from shore, though, we couldn't catch another puff of air for anything, even after I set the jib. The boat sat as quietly on the water as if we'd put down the anchor, which is what I usually liked to do when I got farther out—though not with company I hadn't counted on having.

The silence between us stretched until it actually began to sound like a roar in my ears. Finally, I couldn't stand it anymore. "So, do you like dogs?" I asked as if I were interrogating a suspect about a neighborhood crime.

The question seemed to catch Michael Miller off guard. I studied him closely for evidence of the phobia I hadn't detected yesterday when he stood at the bottom of the stairs.

"Sure," he said. "We had a pooch at home." Drat. It might be harder to get rid of him than the captain of the football team.

"My folks got him for my brother and me at an animal shelter one Christmas." He paused as if he were picturing the dog in his mind's eye. "He was some sort of terrier, a real sweet character. One of those shorthaired little mutts with legs the size of Popsicle sticks. You wondered how they held him up. We named him Toby, and he liked to sleep on the end of my brother's bed. He got to be pretty old—about fifteen, I think—before he died. He had arthritis and his eyebrows had turned gray. That was just before—" He paused, but didn't go on.

"Just before what?" I prodded.

"Never mind," he said with a shrug, and turned away so I could only see his profile etched against the blackness of the pines on the far side of the lake. Silence stretched between us again. *That was just before . . .*

What had he been about to say? Whatever it was, it was evident Michael Miller didn't intend to tell me. Then he turned toward me as if he'd put whatever it was out of his mind and said in a warm, eager way, "She's a real sweetheart, isn't she?"

I patted the *Guinevere* affectionately. Her white deck was smooth and familiar under my palm. "You bet," I agreed. "As sweet as they come. After Dad brought her home we gave her a fresh coat of paint and patched the hole in her starboard side. She's as good as new. I can't see why everyone else in the family got tired of her so quick."

The peanut butter sandwich in my pocket felt a little lumpy and considering that Michael actually seemed to be interested in the *Guinevere*, I wondered if I should offer him half of it. Then I noticed he was smiling at me.

"Your sister, I meant," he said.

Dumbhead. Idiot. Fool. I must've left my brain on the dock. What made me think el boyfriendo really cared a hoot about the *Guinevere*? Had he come home with Kimmy for a whole summer so he could learn how to sail? No. He came to Brookfield to spend as much time as possible with Miss Congeniality.

Any nitwit except Sarah S. Stupido would've known that. No wonder I didn't have a boyfriend. I was too dumb to deserve one, even a shy one like Jason Conrad who was two inches shorter than me, got good grades, and would never know hot from cold.

But since Michael Miller was the one who brought up the subject of Kimmy, I pursued it.

"Kim told Mom and Dad in a letter you guys are thinking about getting married after you graduate. Is that true?" I demanded, as if I were still filling out a police report. I didn't bother to mention the only reason I knew about their plans was because I'd eavesdropped when I was cleaning dog pans. Anyway, if I was going to be his sister-in-law I had a right to know a few more details.

"Well—" Michael rubbed the faded knees of his jeans thoughtfully. Suddenly it occurred to me that maybe he wasn't on fire to do any such thing.

What if getting married was mostly Kim's idea? That

meant it was possible Michael Miller would decide to leave Brookfield before summer was over. It was what I wanted more than anything. Just the same, I couldn't help feeling a little sorry to think how zapped my sister would be when she found out.

"I'd like to," he said slowly. "But getting married isn't something people ought to do lightly. There are lots of things to think about, to talk about." He looked at me with an expression in his eyes I couldn't decode.

Then he asked suddenly, "Do you remember what Merlin told Arthur?"

If I had, I'd forgotten. "'Guinevere will cause you sorrow,' Merlin warned," Michael said softly. "Legend says that every one of Merlin's predictions came true, and that one did too."

It's a funny thing about having a sister. You don't mind ragging on her yourself, but you don't like to have other people do it. "My sister's the happiest person I know, and she doesn't go around making people feel bad," I said in a voice that was louder than it needed to be.

I was about to give him some practical advice—tell him not to rush into anything he wasn't sure about, for instance (right, Sarah Connelly had so much experience in romance she could lecture about such stuff)—when I saw Joey on the dock, waving his skinny white arms over his head. It was too early in the summer for him to have gotten much of a tan yet and he looked like a Halloween skeleton.

"Mom's probably got breakfast ready," I said, pinching up the jib. Finally a puff of air filled it and I tacked for shore.

"You'll have to show me how to do that sometime," Michael said, smiling, as I worked the sails. He had a way of looking straight at a person that was sort of unnerving. As if he were trying to see way down deep inside you, as if you might be hiding something important and he wanted to pull it out of whatever dark cranny you'd stuck it in.

"Don't count on getting any sailing lessons from me," I replied in frosty Siberian tones. "I have to help Dad with the dogs. Mostly, I do the grunt stuff while he does the actual handling. Last year, though, he started to teach me how to handle, and if I can get the grunt stuff done real fast every morning he said he'll work with me some more. So I seriously doubt I'll have any time to spare. Sorry."

Another fib. I wasn't sorry at all. I just hoped it wouldn't take Michael Miller all summer to figure out he didn't really want to marry Kimmy. If it only took him a few more weeks there'd be plenty of time for her to get over the shock of getting dumped before she went back to college. It'd also give me time to have Katie and Camilla out for sleepovers.

"Why didn't you guys wake me up so I could come too?" Joey whined as soon as I tied up at the dock. He wasn't wearing a shirt and his ribs poked up under his pale skin like frail twigs.

"Don't be such a grump," I told him bluntly.

"I'm sorry, Joey," Michael said in a much kinder tone. "Next time, we won't run off without you. Will we, Sarah?"

I didn't answer. The warm, sincere sound in his voice bugged me. I almost believed he truly didn't want to hurt Joey's feelings. The possibility he and Joey might get chummy sure wasn't a thrill. I'd have to remind my brother the reason he couldn't have Skippy Simpson sleep over till school started was because

Michael would probably be around for the entire summer.

As I let the sails down, Michael and Joey headed for the house. Michael laid his arm across Joey's bony white shoulder and I saw my brother look up with a satisfied little smirk. I frowned and patted my shirt pocket. My peanut butter sandwich had gotten kind of flat, but I pulled it out and ate the whole thing as I followed the two of them up to the back porch.

I scowled at their backs. They acted as if they'd been friends forever. *No fair!* I wanted to yell. I'd better work fast or Michael would win Joey over for sure, which—considering my folks already seemed to like Michael just fine—would make me a minority of one.

I got my chance right after breakfast, when Joey went upstairs to make his bed. After I was sure nobody else was within earshot, I reminded Joey why Skippy couldn't come over. He wasn't as upset as I hoped he'd be.

"No big deal," he said airily. "Just means Mom'll let me go over to Skippy's oftener. That's better anyway, because his folks let us stay up later than Mom does. Besides, Michael said he'd show me how to play chess this summer."

"Chess?"

"Sure. He says he's taught kids even younger than me. He said it's a game that was invented in Persia way back in olden times. He said maybe even King Arthur played it."

Arthur, Smarthur. I watched my brother finish making his bed. He didn't actually make it, just kind of flattened the covers out and yanked the bedspread over his pillow. Then I went into Kim's room and plopped down on the rollaway.

Not only were Michael and Joey making buddy plans for the summer, my brother was calling el boyfriendo

Michael in a way that hinted he liked him as much as he did that no-neck Brad-Chad-Tad guy.

No fair! I pressed my pinkie against the spot on my forehead that was still tender from the smack I gave myself on the table yesterday. I knew I was in a war that wasn't going to be easy to win.

chapter four

On Monday, Kim and Michael put the top down on his little green sports car and got ready to head off to town. Kim said she wanted to look up some of her old cronies from high school.

"And of course I want to show off my Cracker Jack prize," she added, smiling at Michael as though she'd just opened a box and there he was, her own precious plastic prince. She matched his stupid lovesickness to perfection; it was vomit comets time again.

"We'll be back whenever," she told Mom, and away they flew, Kim's hair streaming out behind her like a bright banner as they turned the corner on the county road next to our mailbox and headed east.

"With any luck they won't hurry back," I muttered under my breath.

"Now, Sarah," my mother said in her usual patient way. "Try not to be so sour."

I chugalugged my orange juice, gobbled my cereal, then said I was going out to help Dad. I hated the hot, teary feeling behind my eyes. How come nobody understood this was supposed to be the best summer of my entire life? The one just before junior high, when maybe Jason Conrad would come out to watch videos with me?

I got my cleaning stuff out of the cabinet in the kennel shed. For the past three summers it'd been my job to clean the dog runs and hose them down. To some people, it might sound yucky—scooping poop for more than twenty or so mutts—but I didn't really mind.

Kim was one of those who thought it was nasty, and hated it when she was my age. She could hardly wait till she got a job in town. But did anybody hassle her or say she was a sour person just because she didn't like what she didn't like? No. *Notfair, notfair, notfair!* I yelled in that big empty room inside my head where I always hid whenever I was in a serious snit.

Dad called cleaning kennels my apprenticeship. Joey wasn't really old enough yet to take over my job, but I'd been hoping somehow I could spend more time with Dad doing actual dog handling instead of nothing but pooper scooping.

Dad did everything himself now, but the more dogs he got the harder it was for him to give each one the kind of attention it deserved. Even though most of the dogs we boarded were regular mutts who belonged to people on holiday or who were there to be bred, the four pooches that were show dogs took at least an hour of attention apiece every day. Then there was all the other maintenance stuff a kennel owner had to do—mending gates, giving medicine to dogs that needed it, taking care of all the book work.

Dad even talked about hiring someone to help him, but I hoped he wouldn't pick a stranger. I wanted him to pick me. So after my eyes quit burning I worked fast—scooping, brooming, hosing—partly because my ruined summer still bummed me out, partly to get through as quick as I could so I could tell Dad I had some free time.

I checked my watch. I'd finished in two hours flat—
a record. "I'm all through with the kennels," I told him
when I found him down in the mini-showring he'd built
at the end of the kennel shed. "So if you want to give me
some lessons—"

He gave me an apologetic look and tapped the cell
phone he carried in a holster on his hip as if it were a six-
shooter. "I'm sorry, Sarah," he said, "but I just got a call
about a new dog coming in on a flight from Nebraska."
He was into the pickup so quick I didn't even have a
chance to tell him I'd hurried extra fast just so we could
have time to work together.

I watched him drive off, my heart a lump in my chest.
No matter what I did, nothing was working out. All my
bad luck seemed to have started with the arrival of
Michael Miller. So I was extra glad that for the rest of the
day there was no puff of dust in the road, no green sports
car turning at the mailbox announcing the return of my
sister and you-know-who.

"You'll never guess what happened!" Kim exclaimed
when she bounced into the kitchen that evening just as
we were sitting down for supper. Michael trailed in behind her wearing his quirky smile and his helmet of silver hair. I detested the very sight of him and kept my eyes
glued on my plate.

"So don't tell us. Let us enjoy the mystery," I suggested pointedly.

As usual, my sister paid no attention to me. "Michael
and I dropped in at the Kwik Pik and Mr. Hubbell asked
me if I wanted my old job back. Can you believe it? He
had someone all lined up for the summer, but she canceled out on him at the last minute."

"Um, what did you say?" Mom asked as she filled everyone's plate with rice and stir-fry, another one of her low-budget, feed-an-army concoctions.

"I told him yes, of course," Kim chirped happily. "The money will come in handy for all the plans Michael and I are making." She gave el boyfriendo a meaningful glance and snuggled under his armpit. I vowed I'd never look at Jason Conrad that way. He'd probably run for his life if I did. Then I noticed Michael's quirky smile looked a little bit strained.

"You don't seem especially glad Kimmy got her old job back," I observed innocently.

He raised his dark eyebrows. "But I *am* glad!" he exclaimed. "It's just that I wish I could get one too." He lifted one shoulder in a shrug. "I'm new to these parts, though. I can understand why no one's overly enthusiastic about hiring a stranger. There's got to be a lot of local types who'll get on before I'd even be considered."

"How hard have you looked?" My voice was still sugar sweet and filled with fake concern. My mother shot me a look that warned silently, *Better knock it off, Sarah.*

"By golly, Michael, I might have something for you," my dad said as he pushed his stir-fry around his plate searching for the cashews my mother always adds to it. I stared at him in shock. He couldn't be serious. But of course el boyfriendo brightened up immediately.

"What's that, Mr. Connelly?"

"Maybe you'd like to give us a hand out in the kennels this summer. I'm going to be getting a couple new boarders—fact is, I just got a call this morning after you kids left, and I picked one of them up this afternoon." He found a cashew and bit into it. "The other one, a Chessie, will be arriving at the end of the week. Sarah here"—he winked and gestured in my direction, his fork loaded with more stir-fry—"will be glad to show you the ropes."

"Dad!" I squawked. "You didn't even ask me if—"

"Well, I didn't think of it until just this minute, Sarah," he said in his cheerful way. "Then, after you show Michael what he needs to know, it'll give you and me a chance to work together."

Dad's smile faded, and he flashed Michael a practical, no-nonsense look. I hoped he'd had a change of heart. "Mind you," he warned, "it won't be full-time, son, and I can only afford to pay you minimum wage. So if you find something in town that suits you better, why, don't hesitate to grab it."

Son. He was calling Michael son, as if he belonged in the family the same as Joey did. It was plain I was the only Connelly who hadn't welcomed the turkey with open arms.

I sagged in my chair. What Dad just suggested was what I wanted: to be able to spend more time learning how to handle the dogs myself. This was my big chance. All I needed to do was grit my teeth long enough to teach Michael Miller the routine of cleaning kennels, then it'd be me and Dad together.

I chewed a cashew.

I chomped a snow pea.

I crunched a Chinese noodle.

How many options did I have? Zippo. The bottom line was I'd have to teach Michael Miller how to scoop poop.

Michael leaned across the table toward me, an earnest look in his blue eyes. "If it's all right with you, Sarah, it's all right with me." He smiled eagerly, showing lots of square white teeth. "And maybe you'll even tell me what a Chessie is."

"It's short for Chesapeake, as in Chesapeake Bay

retriever," I mumbled. But before I agreed for sure that
I'd teach el boyfriendo anything more than what a
Chessie was, I needed an answer from Dad about an im-
portant question.

"Do you think there's any chance I could work with
Bingo?" I asked.

He gave me a foxy grin. "Now why am I not surprised you asked, Sarah?" he said. "Well, the little bit we
worked together last year showed me you're good with
dogs—quiet and patient and methodical—so I don't see
why you can't."

Quiet. Patient. Methodical. Those three words might
not sound like praise to some people, but that's sure what
they sounded like to me.

Joey leaned his breastbone against the edge of the
table. His chin grazed his stir-fry. "Everybody's got a job
but me," he whimpered, and I heard the mournful sound
of sniffles in his voice. Michael quickly reached out to
stroke my brother's head, then cupped his hand around
the back of Joey's neck, which was pink now with his
first sunburn of the summer.

"Hey, Joey. You can be my assistant, okay? As soon as
Sarah gets me up to speed, then it'll be you and me together, buddy."

Joey blinked back his tears and smiled at Michael like
he'd just been blessed by the hand of God. My parents
looked at the two of them with satisfaction, while Kim
beamed her approval. I concentrated on my plate again.
Everything Michael Miller did seemed, well, thoughtful.
Kind and considerate too. How long could a person keep
on despising someone who was thoughtful, kind, and
considerate?

"Oh, by the way," Kim said brightly, turning to me
with a sly look. "Guess who I saw today at the Kwik Pik?"

"Elvis Presley. He's alive and well and living in Meadowville, right?"

"Almost as exciting," she purred. "Jason Conrad, that's who. He even asked about you."

"He did?" I didn't know whether to be flattered or embarrassed. I'd never talked about Jason to anyone but Katie Albright. "What'd you tell him?"

"That you were fine and had a little spare time on your hands. I invited him to come out some afternoon."

"Kim!" I screeched. How could she do such a thing? I was only *thinking* about Jason Conrad. It wasn't like I was actually ready to *do* anything about him.

She reached over and patted me in a mother-hen way, as if she were a century older than me rather than just a few years. "Not to worry, dear child. He won't be out any time soon," she assured me. "He told me he's going on vacation tomorrow with his folks. To Florida. They'll be gone a month."

Leave it to my mother, though, to notice I still wasn't as thrilled as everyone else about Michael. Because later, when it was just the two of us in the kitchen and I was scraping plates before putting them in the dishwasher, she began to talk about him.

"He really seems like such a nice young man," she began. "At supper I thought it was so sweet the way he tried to make Joey feel important. It's plain it meant a lot to Joey."

"Joey also liked Kim's football player," I reminded her, "and he turned out to have a fo-bee-uh."

"Now, Sarah," my mother murmured as she leaned her backside against the counter and watched me finish loading the dishwasher. She sighed and nibbled her bottom lip. "I don't know exactly how to say this, sweetie, but—"

"Then maybe you shouldn't," I interrupted. Whenever she called me sweetie I knew I was in for some kind of lecture.

"Well, I have to, Sarah. Look, sweetie—" Here it comes, I thought, and resigned myself.

"—the six of us are going to be together all summer, so it's important that we get along," she said. "But if you keep taking potshots at Michael like you did at supper tonight it'll only make everyone uncomfortable. It puts a certain tension in the air that makes all of us uneasy." She fidgeted with the hem of her University of Wisconsin T-shirt before she went on.

"Lots of girls are jealous of an older sister, Sarah. It's quite normal and nothing to be ashamed of. Since I was the only girl in a family of boys, I never had any reason to feel jea—"

"I am *not* jealous of Kim!" I objected. The funny thing was, it was almost the truth. I'd never really minded that Kim looked like a model or had tons of friends. She was a good sister most of the time. She used to rub my back to make me feel better when I was sick. Until lately, I hadn't even minded that she got a pretty name and I had a plain one. Maybe that was because Kim never lorded it over anyone, not even me.

Anyway, I didn't need to look like a model or have the phone ringing for me all the time to be a professional dog handler. All I needed was to have a touch with animals, and Dad had already said in front of the whole family that I was quiet, patient, and methodical.

"But I *do* think things could be just a little more equal around here," I pointed out as I poured soap powder into the dispenser and started the dishwasher. "Everybody takes it for granted that whatever Kim wants, Kim gets."

I eyeballed my mother, who listened to me as if suddenly what I was saying mattered.

"For instance, getting a job in town because she didn't like to clean the kennels. Or inviting someone to spend the whole entire summer without bothering to ask Joey or me if we had any plans."

My mother stopped fussing with the hem of her T-shirt and looked at me apologetically. *Ah!* I knew I'd hit a nerve.

"So if I decide I want to keep Abigail because Camilla's got to move into an apartment that doesn't allow pets after her folks get divorced, will you let me?"

I knew perfectly well cats were my mother's least favorite animal, but I could tell my question made her stop to wonder if she'd always been as fair to me as she thought she was. Since I had the advantage, I decided to press on to victory.

"The thing is, Mom, nobody would've had a problem if el boyfriendo had come to stay for two weeks. A month, even. But *the whole summer?* I mean, you gotta admit it's a bit much."

She sighed. "I wish you wouldn't call him el boyfriendo, Sarah. It sounds rude and insulting. Almost as bad as calling him a turkey."

"Well, that's how I feel, Mom. Rude. Insulting. Bent out of shape. You get the picture."

"I certainly do," she agreed. "But maybe after you've had a chance to work with Michael for a while you'll change your mind about him." She reached out and pulled me against her for a quick hug. I didn't resist. In fact, I leaned against her and hung on. My mother's as solid and comforting as a tree whose roots go way down deep.

"And I'm sorry I said you were jealous, Sarah." She

patted me as if she were burping a baby. "I guess it was
my imagination working overtime. You and Kim have
always been the best of sisters, even though there's quite
a difference in your ages. Just forget what I said, okay?"

I hugged her back. I don't like the feeling of being
mad at somebody. Even el boyfriendo. It ruins everything. My mother kissed me on the tender spot on my
forehead, which made me feel a little better. However,
that didn't mean my daily dose of conversation about
Michael Miller was over yet.

Because that night as Kim and I got into bed—she in
her comfy, spacious one under an open window, me in
my lumpy, little one in a dark airless corner—she said it
really bothered her that I didn't seem to like Michael
better.

"He's only been here a few days. I hardly know the
guy yet," I explained. "Maybe it'll be like Mom says.
After we've worked together awhile I'll learn to like him
the same way the rest of you guys do."

"I hope so, Sarah, because Michael really means a lot
to me," Kim said. She sighed and flopped around in her
bed to get more comfortable. "Michael is, well, he's special, Sarah. His life has been, um, kind of hard. He's a
person who needs a lot of TLC and—"

"What's been so hard about his life?" I asked when
she paused in midsentence. "He drives a sports car. He
goes to a great college. He has a gorgeous girlfriend.
Mom said he comes from a fine family. It's not exactly
like he's underprivileged, so what's all this stuff about
TLC?"

"Michael needs to feel welcome here because, um,
well, Sarah, I don't think his parents really understand
how sensitive he is. See, some real serious stuff has gone
down with Michael. Stuff that worries him a lot and

makes him think he's not as good a person as I know he really is."

"Why don't his folks understand him? What kind of serious stuff?" I was beginning to get interested.

"Just stuff. It's hard to explain."

"Are you sure you know what you're talking about, Kim?"

"Of course I do," she said. "The point is, Sarah, when we get married he'll be a permanent part of the family and it'll be awkward to say the least if my very own sister can't stand the person who's my husband."

It was plain Kim didn't know yet that Michael might not be as crazy about getting married as she thought he was. On the other hand, what if he did eventually get to be a fixture in the family?

Kim was right. It'd be a real problem if I couldn't learn to get along with him. I might end up like Mom's friend, Sarah Williams. I'd have to leave the country. I tried to figure out where I'd like to go. The truth was, I couldn't think of a nicer place to be than Wisconsin, especially in the summer, surrounded by pine trees, listening to loons on Echo Lake, learning to handle a dog like Bingo.

"Kim?"

"What?" she asked. I could tell she was getting sleepy.

"I promise I'll try to like him better." Maybe I could afford to practice a little charity. Because I might not have to do it very long. Not if Michael Miller decided sooner rather than later that he really didn't want to get married after all.

chapter five

Once, Dad told me dogs are able to pick up on things about a person that humans can't. He said they have sort of a sixth sense about emotions like fear or disgust or meanness.

The mutts in the kennels sure picked up vibes from Kim, for instance. They knew she thought poop was loathsome. That cold, wet noses or warm, slobbery tongues totally disgusted her. So when she had my job, they slouched around her with apologetic looks, their ears flattened to their heads, their tails tucked between their legs, and kept from getting too close to her.

Now that I'm the one who takes care of them, though, they all act witlessly gleeful every time I show up. So I figured how the pooches took to Michael would give me a good read on him. I regretted to observe they took to him the same way the whole Connelly family had.

After letting them take a good smell of his hand— and he held it out to them the right way, balled up in a fist, not with fingers extended, which can scare a dog that doesn't know you—Michael had a way of rubbing their ears or scratching under their jaws that seemed to please them. Darn. I'd almost hoped they'd bare their teeth at him and get that ominous look in their eyes that meant they were ready to snap.

For about the tenth time I reminded myself of the bargain I'd made with Dad. Training Michael would give me a chance to work with Bingo. Get with the program, Sarah, I told myself. Forget about this guy taking a three-month lease on your room.

"First, we take each pooch out of its individual run and put it over there in the holding pen," I explained, pointing toward the end of the kennel shed. We only moved two dogs at a time, tying them up at opposite ends of the pen so they wouldn't get in any kind of a tussle.

"Then, since today's Friday, we'll put disinfectant in the wash water when we hose down the runs."

Michael watched as I pulled on a pair of rubber gloves, measured some cloudy stuff out of a green bottle into the dispenser—the same kind gardeners use for spraying vegetables with herbicide—then hooked it onto the nozzle of a hose.

Next, I showed him how to collect poop with a plastic scooper and drop it into a bucket with cat litter in the bottom. Later, I'd show him the lime pit out behind the shed where we dumped the droppings. Then I demonstrated how to wash off the concrete slab in front of the dog's shelter with a blast from the hose. After the pens were washed down, I showed Michael how to take a broom and sweep the water off the concrete slab in front of each dog's house and into a trough that ran the length of the kennel shed and emptied into a drain at the far end.

"How'm I doing, Sarah?" he asked with a grin, when by midmorning I hadn't lavished any high praise on him or remarked on his amazing talent with a broom.

"Good enough," I mumbled.

Michael and I finished the runs—twenty-three of them—without any other chitchat. Then, as he brushed diligently at the floor of the last one, his blue T-shirt showing half-moons of sweat under the arms, he paused and leaned on his broom.

"Sarah, there's something I want to talk to you about," he began.

Oh, great. I shot a glance in his direction. Suspicion tightened steel bands around my chest. I'd had too many lectures lately from Mom and Kim. For sure I didn't need another one from a person who was basically a stranger.

"I want to thank you for giving up your room to me for the summer," Michael said. He must've been a mind reader, because even though I wanted to forget that fact, my blasted vacation had been uppermost in my mind as we'd worked silently side by side all morning.

"I realize it was no small sacrifice for you to turn it over to me, Sarah. I just want you to know I really appreciate it. Like they say, now I owe you one."

His next remark surprised me even more. He looked at me, laughing, his blue eyes crinkly at the corners, his sleek silver hair flopping over his sweaty forehead, and said, "By the way, have you ever noticed the water stains on your ceiling? One of them makes me think of the head of a wild mustang I saw once in a photograph in *National Geographic*."

"Huh! I thought it looked more like a dog's," I countered. Who knows why people tell such outright fibs? It had *always* reminded me of a horse's head. A mustang's at that, even though I'd never seen the *National Geographic* photograph he was talking about. Just the same, knowing Michael Miller saw exactly the same thing I did made me feel a little friendlier toward him.

"I like that view out your window too," he went on as he finished brushing the rinse water out of the last pen and into the trough. "A person can look right out on Echo Lake and see the *Guinevere* at the dock. That dark line of pines along the opposite shore too. It's a pretty sight, no matter whether it's the last thing at night or the first thing in the morning. And the sound of the loons— that's something, isn't it?"

Loons call back and forth to each other in such a mournful way that even if you're not sad it sort of tugs at your heart.

"The Indians who first lived in this part of Wisconsin had a story about how the loon got its necklace of white feathers," I said. Michael looked at me expectantly.

"Tell it to me," he urged. "I like old stories like that."

"Well, this family had two children, a boy and a girl. But they hid the boy away to keep the evil spirits from harming him. His sister—she was called Loon Woman—never knew of his existence. When she grew up, Loon Woman heard someone call from across the lake. She was enchanted by the sound, and pledged to love forever the creature who'd made it." I didn't go on. I felt nervous talking about love to a person such as Michael Miller.

"And then what?" he prompted.

"Um, Loon Woman found out it belonged to her very own brother. She took him away from his hiding place, but then he was killed by evil spirits. Afterward, she found his heart broken into lots of little pieces, and made a necklace for herself to remind her of her one and only love."

I thought I'd never get to the end of it. Telling stories

about love and evil spirits and hearts broken in pieces
isn't my thing. I wished I'd never brought it up.

"What a terrific story, Sarah," Michael said. "I'm glad
you told it to me." The way he said it I knew he wasn't
putting me on.

I watched him flick the last of the wash water off his
broom and imagined him behind the door of *my* room,
resting his elbows on *my* windowsill, leaning out *my* window morning and evening, listening to the loons across
the lake. Maybe talking about love did something weird
to me, because it seemed as if a pinhole opened somewhere on my skin. With a whoosh, some of my spite
leaked away like air out of a balloon.

A half hour earlier I still hadn't liked him much. But
with that remark about the horse's head and talking
about Loon Woman he didn't seem quite as much like an
interloper anymore. Mrs. Graham encouraged us to
work on our vocabulary over the summer, and "interloper" was a word I'd looked up yesterday. It meant
someone who intruded on the rights or privileges of another person. Which is definitely how I'd thought of him.

We put the brooms and buckets, the disinfectant and
the hose away in the utility shed. I checked my watch. It
wasn't noon yet. "You want to know which one of these
mutts is my favorite?" I asked. My new mood almost
made me nice.

I motioned Michael to follow me down the aisle of
the shed to run number 17. Bingo pressed eagerly against
the gate and I stuck my fingers through the chain-link
fence so he could slobber on them.

"Meet Bingo. Of course, that's only his nickname.
When he came to Brookfield, Dad checked him out right
away—his height, weight, conformation, the way he
moved—then he said, 'Bingo! I think we've got ourselves

a winner here.'" I told Michael all the stuff I knew by heart: where Labradors came from, how they'd been a fisherman's dog that dragged nets up onto the beach, what Bingo's real name was—until I noticed him smiling at me. I knew I'd rattled on too much.

"Can we take him out for a while?" he asked when I quit yakking. "I'd like to see how you train a dog like Bingo."

I hesitated. I'd never worked with Bingo myself. "We'll just give him some ordinary exercise, okay? Dad's already got Bingo on a training schedule, and I don't want to do anything that might mess 'im up."

"Do you—" Michael hesitated a moment. His eyes seemed to darken. "Do you train them with . . . with guns?"

"Guns?"

"A Labrador's a retriever, right? I mean, Bingo's a hunting dog, so I figured—"

"Sure he is, but at Brookfield we do show dog training, not field training." I clipped a lead onto Bingo's blue nylon collar.

Michael sighed, as if he were relieved. "Dad used to hunt pheasants and ducks himself, but he got so busy he had to give up the sport," I said. "So—are you a hunter?" Michael kept his face turned away and didn't answer.

We walked Bingo around the exercise yard, and I did some sit, stay, down exercises with him. I showed Michael how to do them too, then we put Bingo back in his run. I saw that it still wasn't noon. Once Mom got home from town it'd take her half an hour to get lunch on. I shaded my eyes with my fingers and squinted at the lake.

"Maybe there's time for a sailing lesson," I suggested. The invitation was out of my mouth before I knew I intended to give it. It surprised me as much as it did Michael.

"No kidding? Say, I'd really like that, Sarah!"

There's one thing I have to honestly admit. Right from the get go, when he stood in the entryway looking up at me, I liked the way Michael Miller said my name. There wasn't any hint of now Sarah or sour Sarah about it. It was almost enough to make me wonder if I wanted to change it to Darla or Raquel or Natalee after all.

We were halfway to the dock when Michael halted abruptly. "Whoa! What about Joey?" he asked. "Remember, I promised him if we went out—"

"He's in town with Mom, getting groceries and picking up a shipment of dog chow," I said. "We can take him with us next time." Wonder of wonders. Being nicer to Michael might even make me more generous with my own flesh and blood.

I showed Michael the right way to push off from the dock, how to lower the centerboard, and the proper way to handle the tiller. The air was light, as it often is in the middle of the day, maybe three or four miles an hour. Just perfect for teaching somebody how to work the sails.

"What did you say about a glacier spring out there in the middle of the lake?" Michael asked as we caught a puff and moved easily across the water.

"I didn't say anything except that's where it's at."

"You said it was really cold," he reminded me.

"It is. Someone told Dad maybe it comes from an ancient glacier way up over the border in Canada. It might be true, because for sure the water out there feels as cold as ice. That's why everyone who swims in Echo Lake stays pretty close to shore." The wind shifted and I tacked for the middle of the lake, then uncleated the sails as we neared it.

"I don't think anyone knows for sure how far it is to the bottom out here," I said, "but we call the middle of the lake the Deep." With her sails limp and the centerboard up, the *Guinevere* began to turn in slow, lazy circles.

"You know what I've always thought about when I'm out here, knowing a spring from ancient times is right under me?" I asked.

Michael waited for me to go on, the edge of his profile etched sharply against the darkness of the pines across the lake. "Like I'm over the center of the world, that's what." I laughed, because it seemed sort of a silly idea. "It's just this crazy feeling I have."

"Oh, maybe it's not so crazy," Michael said in the mild, thoughtful way I was almost getting used to. "Actually, that's a common belief in many different cultures. You know, that there *is* a center of the world, and that it's the best place a person could be. And would you believe it just happens to be right where a person's at? Social scientists have a fancy word for it. They call it 'ethnocentrism.'"

I filed that word away in my head; it'd be a good one to add to my vocabulary collection. Michael stared off toward the far shore, but I invited him to look over the edge of the *Guinevere*.

"See how dark the water is? Once upon a time, I guess there wasn't a lake here yet, only that glacier spring bubbling up in the middle of a deep valley. Then, a couple hundred years ago, water flooded this area and covered the trees that were growing here. Dad says wood doesn't rot very fast in water as cold as this, so maybe those trees are still down there."

I peered at my own wavy reflection, but still Michael didn't look down. He kept his gaze trained on the distant shore.

"There's an old story about someone going across the lake in a leaky boat in a storm," I said. "That was way back before there were diving suits or anything like that. Nobody could figure out how to bring the man up again, so they never did."

Even then, Michael didn't look down. "It's kind of spooky to think about," I mused. "Maybe those ancient trees have their branches still raised up to the sun. They might be holding that guy in their arms. It's one of those spooky stories that's kinda cool to think about."

Slowly, almost as if he were afraid he might see white bones cradled in submerged tree branches, Michael leaned over the side of the *Guinevere*. Above us, there were no clouds and the sky was its usual deep blue, but none of the color was reflected in the black water over the Deep where the boat drifted.

"Who was it?" Michael asked. His voice was thin, as if he'd been only half listening to what I said, as if he'd heard something entirely different.

"Who was who?"

"Who was the person who drowned here?"

"Beats me. It's just a story," I said. "Who knows if it's even true? Maybe someone just made it up. You know how it is with stories like that. Maybe that's even how the stories about King Arthur and Loon Woman got started. They just got told so often people believed they were real."

I trailed my fingers in the water. It was so cold my hand burned. "Feel it. Like ice water," I said. Michael did, then drew his hand out as quickly as I had.

Then I showed Michael how to pinch up the sails tighter and we moved cleanly toward shore. The silence that fell between us wasn't the noisy, roaring kind it'd been a few days ago. Finally, Michael said in a weird way, like a person who's just waking up out of a dream, "Do you have any idea how lucky you are, Sarah?"

"Lucky?"

Lots of times I didn't feel that way. Like when I only got a C in health science even though the night before I studied almost till midnight for the exam.

Michael glanced up at the sky. It may have been blue, but to me his eyes looked even bluer. "Think about it. You've got a wonderful family," he said. "A terrific sister, a neat brother, fantastic parents. Kim's told me so much about all of you, and here you are—all of you—living at the center of the world."

I had the feeling I should say something important, but I couldn't think of anything. So I said the first thing that came to my mind.

"Well, you're here, Michael. Maybe that means you're lucky too."

He turned to me with a smile that wasn't really a smile at all but another quirky upturning of the corners of his mouth, just like the day I leaned over the bannister to scope him out for signs of a phobia. Except this time I saw a look behind his blue eyes that I'd never seen in the eyes of any person I'd ever known. Not in Katie's eyes or Joey's or Kim's or my parents'. For sure not Jason Conrad's. It had something to do with a kind of sorrow that's too big to measure.

"Maybe you're right, Sarah," he whispered. "Maybe I'm lucky too. Kimberlee . . . Joey . . . you . . . your folks . . . even Bingo. With all of you here at Brookfield I feel like—well, just an ordinary guy."

What made him *not* ordinary? I wondered. Did having a father who operated on people's hearts make Michael so special that he didn't feel like a regular person?

"And you know something else, Sarah?" I waited for him to tell me.

"Now that I've met all of you I want to marry Kim more than ever."

So I'd been wrong. He *did* want to get married. The look in Michael Miller's eyes should've been joy, which would've been natural considering he'd just told me how lucky he was and how he wanted to marry Kim more than anything in the world. Except that's not what I saw.

There was a peculiar sad shadow behind the blueness, something that for a minute made his eyes much less blue than the bottle above my mother's kitchen sink. As I watched, Michael Miller's eyes became almost as dark as the water over the Deep.

The back of my neck suddenly felt cool. "Bet Mom and Joey are home by now," I said. "Let's go see what's for lunch. I hope she bought some wieners and buns so we can make chili dogs with cheese."

I was relieved to see the water beneath us turn a lighter color as we left the cold darkness and the submerged trees of the Deep behind us.

chapter six

A week later, after Kim hopped into Michael's little green car and tootled off for her early shift at the Kwik Pik, Dad asked me at breakfast how Michael was coming along with my old kennel job. Across the table I saw Michael lower his glance and butter a second piece of toast as he waited for me to answer.

"He's doing great, Dad." For a change, I didn't mumble or talk to my plate. I looked straight at Dad and said it like I meant it.

"He seems to have no problems with the somewhat unsavory aspects of scooping poop?" Dad winked at Michael and smiled in the lopsided way he has that can put at ease even hunky football players who've been scared out of their wits by poodles.

"No problems," I assured him. "Not like some people I could mention." I didn't mention I was thinking of Kim.

"Well, why don't you start back to work with me this morning, Sarah? We'll begin with that new Chessie. She doesn't seem as hardheaded as a lot of Chesapeakes I've handled, and has settled down nicely after her flight.

We'll work her together, till you understand exactly what
I expect from her—and *you*."

He took another gulp of coffee, clapped his Green
Bay Packers cap on his head, and headed for the back
door. "Meet me in the exercise yard behind the shed as
soon as you've finished with breakfast," he called over his
shoulder.

There was something I had to know before I followed him, though. "Is it okay with you?" I asked
Michael. Because I hadn't been about to put out of my
mind the weird look I saw in his eyes when he talked
about being lucky, about being a regular person, about
the center of the world being wherever a person's at. I
needed to know if he was all right with being turned
loose to clean kennels by himself.

"You said Joey could help you, and since he already
knows a lot of the stuff he'll be good company for you," I
reminded him.

"Yeah!" Joey exclaimed, before Michael had a chance
to speak up himself. "I know Sarah's job practically by
heart, even though Dad said I was too little yet to do it
myself. Anything you need to know, Michael, just ask
me. We'll be a team, like you promised."

Michael grinned and gave Joey an elbow in the ribs.
"You got it, buddy." Joey looked at him with a worship-
ful expression, but this time his goofy adoration didn't in-
spire me to upchuck. Actually, I was beginning to be glad
he liked Michael so well.

"Now it's my turn to have you," Joey said smugly, as
if Michael were a piece of merchandise everyone in the
family had to learn to share, like we all had to learn to
share the *Guinevere*. "Till now, it's been you and Kim together all the time, or else Sarah's been the one who had
you."

I felt my cheeks get warm. "You aren't too little to have scooped poop anytime you wanted, mister," I retorted. "Don't make it sound like I hogged Michael all to myself."

"Stop, you two," my mother said in the absentminded way she has when she wants to remind Joey and me we're brother and sister. It was plain Michael and Joey were satisfied with the arrangement, so I gobbled the rest of my toast and headed after Dad.

The Chessie's owners had the same grand expectation for her that Bingo's did for him—that eventually she might win Best of Breed at Westminster—or even better, maybe a Best of Show. Once she did, they'd set her to raising pups, for which they'd be guaranteed to get fancy prices.

Dad already had Chessie out of her pen when I caught up with him. She was a good-size dog, her coat the color of dead grass, which sounds ugly and dull but actually was sort of pretty. That dead grass color is important, because Chesapeakes are a duck-retrieving dog and are supposed to be as close as possible to the color of the autumn marshes they'd be working in. She was registered as Gatsby's Golden Girl, but since Dad was already in the habit of calling her Chessie, he just kept right on and I did too.

"One of our big jobs with this young lady might be keeping her coat in shape," Dad pointed out. "Look at this—" He plucked at her shoulders. "There's just a little too much curl here. Her coat should have a bit of a wave in it but no actual kinkiness. We'll be careful about the way we groom her and maybe we can tease it into shape."

But it was Bingo I really wanted to talk about. "D'you think there'll be some time this morning for us to work with Bingo a little bit?" I asked. I thought how cheerful he'd been with Michael and me a few days ago. There was something steady about Bingo too. He made me think of the kind of hero dogs you see in Disney movies, the ones you can trust with your life if you need to.

"We'll see, Sarah. I've been having some trouble with him and I want to be very careful I don't mess him up even worse. It's true he's got all the earmarks of a champion, but he's also got some unexpected hang-ups."

"Hang-ups?" I was startled. He'd never mentioned anything about Bingo's troubles or hang-ups before.

"Turns out there's an awfully shy streak in him," Dad went on. "For example, just for the heckuvit I took him down near the lake—and found out he's water shy, if you can believe it! Which makes it just as well the colonel wants him show trained, not field trained, because I have a hunch Bingo-boy might turn out to be worthless in that department. But even with showring basics, I've noticed Bingo has sort of a gloomy manner—not the upbeat, cheerful behavior a show dog's gotta have to be a winner." He sighed. "It just means we'll have to be careful not to push him too hard right now."

I thought of how agreeable Bingo was with Michael and me, and wondered if Dad could've been mistaken. Then, as if worry about Bingo wasn't enough, Dad was in for another surprise. Chessie turned out to be as tough and hardheaded as they come.

"She's been spoiled by experiences she can't tell us about," Dad said as he tried to get her to heel. "What makes a Chesapeake a fine water dog—their tough, resourceful nature—is the very thing that also makes them hard to train if you don't get 'em started off on the right foot."

Chessie pulled back hard on the leash, bracing her forelegs as if she intended to turn the session into a battle of wills. But Dad never scolded her. Instead, he rubbed her ears and told her she was a good girl, then tried again. Grudgingly, she finally followed him across the exercise yard with a stiff-legged gait that was anything but the loose, easy movement that looks good in a showring.

"There's generally two ways to train a Chessie," he said. "You can handle 'em tender or you can handle 'em tough. It's not the end of the world that she's stubborn today," he told me as we walked back to the kennel shed. "We'll go with tenderness first, and hope her attitude's just that she hasn't gotten used to Brookfield yet. For now, there's no sense humiliating her." He passed her lead to me.

"Put her back in her pen, Sarah, while I go in and grab another cup of coffee. Then you can get that little Dandie Dinmont terrier out and take him down to the arena."

Joey and Michael were laughing up a storm at the far end of the shed as I put Chessie away, and for the first time I understood what my mother meant about how important it was for us to get along because we were all going to be together for the summer. For a change, it didn't seem so horrible that Jason Conrad hadn't come out, or that Katie couldn't sleep over.

Chessie may have been a pain but Randolph's Roman Candle was a stitch. He thought he was such hot stuff that it was a tickle to put him through his paces. Some dogs love to be looked at, love to entertain an audience, and Randy was one of them.

There are two parts to showing a dog, gaiting and stacking, and Randy already knew how to do both. Dad went through the routine first, then set me to work. First, I stacked him. Basically, that means training a dog how to hold a pose: making sure he's got his best side to the judge, neck outstretched, head up, feet positioned just so. Randy loved to pose, and he rolled his eyes sideways at me as if to say, *"Ain't I just the cat's pajamas?"*

Then I gaited him around the arena Dad had built at the end of the shed. It was a smaller version of a professional showring. I trotted Randy around in a circle, in a back-and-forth pattern, then in an *L,* which would give a judge a chance to get a good look at how he turned corners coming and going.

When I was done, Dad threw an arm around my shoulder. "By golly, you remembered everything I showed you last year!" he exclaimed. "You're gonna make a proud old man out of your dad one of these days." I hugged him and laid my ear over his heart. He smelled of sweat and dog hair, which were like perfume to me.

Michael was right. I *was* lucky.

That night, after Kim and Michael got back from a long walk around the lake, we crawled into bed and she turned off the light. I lay on my lumpy cot and thought how different things were compared to when Michael first came to Brookfield. I smiled in the dark, glad instead of mad for a change.

I got to wondering if the easy touch Michael had with dogs had anything to do with the little stray with legs like Popsicle sticks that his folks got from the animal shelter when he and his brother were kids. What was the pooch's name? Yeah, Toby. I lifted myself up on one elbow.

"Hey, Kim? You asleep?" I called over to her.

"Not yet," she murmured groggily. If I'd waited another minute she would've been zonked.

"Michael told me how he and his brother got a dog for Christmas when they were kids," I said. "It died after it got pretty old. By then, it had gray eyebrows and arthritis. They named it Toby and it liked to sleep on the end of his brother's bed. Only Michael never told me if his brother was older or younger."

I hoped he was younger, about my age. If Kim and Michael got married after graduation, I'd probably meet him at the wedding. I'd wear a dress instead of ratty jeans or shorts. Mom could help me do something with my burlap hair. It would be sort of romantic. I imagined telling Katie and Camilla about it.

"Listen, you guys, you won't believe what Michael's brother looks like. To die for. Almost like a movie star. He likes me too." Which might not be the truth. *"We're going to start writing letters back and forth."* Which probably wouldn't be true either. Just the same, I could imagine the pinched, envious looks on their faces.

"I think he was, um, a couple years older," Kim answered.

"What's his name?" I persisted when she didn't go on.

"Um, Matthew." Michael and Matthew. Cool names for two brothers. Biblical, kind of.

"Is Matthew in college too?"

"Um, no." Her voice had a detached, let's-not-talk-about-Michael's-brother sound, but I paid no attention to it.

"So has he graduated already?"

"No."

"What's he do then? Does he still live at home like Camilla's big brother, Reuben?"

"No."

Okay, so Matthew didn't go to college and he didn't live at home. "Where does he work? What kind of a job does he have? Does he have his own apartment or what?"

"For heaven's sake, Sarah!" Kim exclaimed, wide awake now, jerking her covers this way and that as she tried to get comfortable again. "Quit being such an infernal pest! We were busy at the Kwik Pik today and I'm tired. Go to sleep. Don't make such a big deal out of Michael's brother." She flopped on her other side, as if to say our conversation was over.

It definitely wasn't my sister's style to use words like "infernal" or "pest," even when she was talking about me.

"Well, ex*cuse* me!" I huffed. "Only I don't know what the big mystery's about. What'd the guy do, shoot somebody and end up in prison?"

The words weren't out of my mouth before I was sorry I'd said them. It could be something just as bad. What if Michael's brother were in a different kind of institution? What if he'd been born with a birth defect and the family couldn't take care of him at home? What if he were one of those people whose bodies grow up but their minds never do and they stay about two years old forever?

There was only silence from the other bed. I figured Kim had gone to sleep. I decided not to ask any more questions anyway, since she was so crabby. Maybe she thought I was prying. Just when I'd given up finding out anything, Kim said in a thin, stretched-out voice, "Michael's brother is dead, Sarah. Michael's the only one in his family now. For him, it's not like it is with you and me and Joey. You know, the three of us together all our lives."

Dead. That's one of those words that doesn't leave any doubt in your mind about what it means. A word like "sick" or "disabled" means there's a future. But *dead* has a built-in end to it. It's a bottom-of-the-sea, deep-in-the-ground kind of word.

I sat up on the rollaway. I could see Kim's eyes were

wide open. She was looking out the window, her face pale green in the glow of the security light Dad had mounted on the kennel shed to flood the yard outside. She seemed to be thinking hard about something.

"So what happened to Michael's brother?" I asked in a voice as soft and thin as hers.

She didn't answer.

"Did he get sick or have some weird disease or what?"

"He died in an accident."

"A car accident?"

"No."

"What kind, then? On a motorcycle?" She didn't answer.

"Did he have a heart attack?" I sounded like a detective again.

"Because there's this kid at school, Eddie Ripley, whose brother had a heart attack last year during a basketball game, even though he was only seventeen. He played center. He died before they could get him off the court. The next day there was a big article about it in the *Gazette* telling how people any age can have what's called silent heart disease. Grief counselors came to school to talk to everyone during a special assembly. It was really sad. Lots of kids cried. I did too."

"Michael's brother was killed in an accident, Sarah."

"You already said that, Kim." I was beginning to get exasperated. "Only you didn't say what kind."

"In an accident with a gun. A rifle."

"He got killed in a hunting accident?" So that's why Michael sounded relieved when he found out Brookfield dogs were trained for the showring, not for the field.

"You mean it was a hunting accident?" I prodded.

"Did Matthew go hunting like Dad used to before he got too busy training so many mutts?"

"Not exactly."

"What's that supposed to mean, 'not exactly'?"

"He was shot accidentally."

"Someone shot Michael's brother accidentally?"

"Yes."

"Who?"

"Michael did, Sarah."

"What?" I must not have heard her right.

"Michael accidentally shot and killed his brother, Sarah."

"Michael . . . killed . . . *his own brother?*"

We'd been talking so softly, almost in whispers, but the words ricocheted off the walls of Kim's room as if she'd screamed them at me.

"When did it happen?"

"Last summer. Before I met Michael." I waited for her to go on. When she did, her voice sounded small and far away.

"Matthew got a rifle for his birthday. One day the guys went out to target practice. The rifle was on the backseat of the car. Matthew opened the door on the driver's side while Michael opened the one on the passenger's side." She paused and took a deep breath.

"Michael reached for it first and it went off somehow. It wasn't even supposed to be loaded. It was one of those freaky accidents you hear about on the evening news. The kind that aren't supposed to happen to anyone you know."

Then I understood why there was a shadow behind Michael's eyes when he talked about how lucky I was to have Kim and Joey. Because he didn't have a brother of his own anymore.

"Michael believes his folks blame him for what happened," Kim said. "Matthew never got a chance to become a doctor, like his folks wanted him to be. Michael says they still keep pictures of him up all over the house, like nothing ever happened. Matthew's room has been left just like it was the last day he was alive. As if any minute he might come walking through the door and life would go on like it always had."

All the time we were out there in the middle of the lake, Michael must've been thinking about Matthew. That it was his fault Matthew was gone. That because of him, Matthew would never meet a girl like Kim and have a chance to get married.

"Sometimes he cries when we walk around the lake," Kim said.

"Michael cries?"

"About Matthew. About what happened. About being the one who's responsible. It's hard for him to forget. It makes him depressed, and when we're alone he talks about it a lot. Sometimes it's the *only* thing he talks about."

I imagined tears in Michael's blue eyes. I wondered if he ever cried till he hiccuped, like I did sometimes.

"Hey, Kim?"

"What?"

"Listen, I'm glad you told me, okay?" All of a sudden the room seemed kind of cold. I hugged myself. "Did you tell Mom and Dad too?" I whispered.

"I'm going to," Kim said in a way that made me understand I wasn't supposed to say anything till she did. "I just didn't want them to get the wrong impression about Michael till they'd had a chance to meet him. It's not like he meant to do anything bad. What happened was just—just an accident."

I didn't bug her anymore. I scrunched down on my cot and thought about Michael across the hall in my room. Was he in bed right now? Or was he leaning across my windowsill, looking into the diamond-pocked sky to study the stars, listening to the mournful call of the loons across the lake? Would that sound make him remember Matthew and start to cry?

I pulled my sheet up to my chin. Nothing could ever make me hate Michael Miller again. I was glad he'd come to Brookfield, far away from anything that reminded him of the terrible thing that happened to his brother. Once they'd been a pair, Michael and Matthew, like brothers in a story. Now Michael was all alone. For the first time I was happy I gave him my room. Even for the whole summer.

chapter seven

Have you ever noticed how once you find out something really big and important about a person they never look exactly the same to you again?

After Katie told me it was true her sister, Emily, was pregnant—just like everybody at school whispered she was—to me, Emily didn't look like an eleventh-grade girl anymore. All of a sudden she seemed grown-up. She knew stuff everybody else wouldn't know for a long time. Scary stuff, like how it felt to have a baby grow inside you, and what would happen once it got ready to be born.

To be honest, knowing what I did about Emily made her look o-l-d. Her eyes, which had always been as brown and twinkly as Katie's, looked regretful. As if she'd accidentally stepped over an invisible line she didn't know was there, then couldn't figure out how to get back across it to the place she used to be.

I was afraid that's exactly how it'd be with Michael.

That after what Kim told me he'd look so different I'd hardly recognize him. That whenever I was around him— which would be every day for the rest of the summer—I'd see somebody who was about to crumble like a soggy cookie because he'd caused a terrible accident that he could never make unhappen. I was afraid I'd never see anything but shadows behind his eyes.

I decided to be extra careful around him. I didn't want to say anything dumb that might make him carry on the way Joey did when his pet gerbil, Sylvester, keeled over on his exercise wheel. Joey cried for two days after he found Sylvester lying there on his back, his little feet in the air, as lifeless as a cold baked potato.

But I didn't have to worry. Michael turned out to be made of tougher stuff. He proved it a couple weeks after Kim told me about what happened to Matthew.

The day started out as usual. Kim went off early to the Kwik Pik and the three of us—Michael, Joey, and I—were getting ready to go outside to work when the phone rang. After Dad hung up, he announced he had to make another quick trip into Meadowville.

"There's another Lab coming in this morning and I want to be right there when it arrives." He wagged his head like a man who's got too much on his plate. I knew what he was thinking, because I'd heard him say it before: *"A show dog trainer's life is feast or famine."* Sometimes you didn't have enough dogs to handle to make a decent living—but with the Chessie and the other new dog, plus the four already on board, Dad knew he'd be putting in sixteen-hour days.

"This is absolutely the last new trainee I'll be able to take for the rest of the year," he told us. "Even with Sarah working with me full-time right up till school starts, we'll be pressed to the max to do right by the ones we've already contracted to handle."

He fixed Joey and Michael with a frown, not because he was mad at them, but because it annoyed him to have to interrupt his schedule again. "You boys take care of your business as usual, and make sure that kennel at the end, number 25, is ready to be occupied." He zeroed in on me. "Sarah, take Bingo out and put him through his yard exercises, just like I showed you the other day."

It was the first time he'd asked me to do it all by myself, which made me feel partly proud and partly nervous. What he didn't know was I'd already taken Bingo out by myself to show off in front of Michael. Dad gave my shoulder a light, guy-type poke, thinking it was my first time.

"You'll do fine, Sarah," he said. "Just remember Bingo's got that timid streak you and I talked about. It's important to make him feel proud of himself, so treat him well. If I'm not back by the time you're done, you can try working that knot-headed Chessie too."

Dad had a rule that he'd drilled into everyone in the family—even Kim, who didn't really like dogs—till we all knew it by heart: Nothing bad should ever happen to a Brookfield dog that would make it mistrust a human being.

Not only was it humane, but harsh treatment could make even the finest dog permanently reluctant to obey commands, which would ruin Dad's reputation as a trainer. So even Chessie could count on being treated well, though one day I heard Dad mutter under his breath that her head was so hard he was tempted to knock some sense into it with a hammer.

Joey and Michael got their brooms, buckets, and hoses, and I picked Bingo's collar and lead off the Peg-Board behind the door of the kennel shed. Dad never put a choke chain on a dog like Bingo. He said there was nothing worse for a tender-spirited dog than a choke chain or a pinch collar, though he admitted he might eventually have to use something like that on Chessie.

When I walked down the aisle of the kennel shed, every dog rushed to the gate of its pen and tuned up. We tried to exercise even the boarders to keep them in good shape, so every dog hoped it was its turn. Bingo usually wasn't a big noisemaker, though. He just came eagerly to his gate and wagged his ropy black tail good-naturedly when I called his name.

"Bingo Chingo Dingo! How's my boy? You gonna do your stuff for me today?" He begged for a head rub by leaning so hard against my leg I had to brace myself against his gate. He might've been timid in spirit, but even though he was only a year old he was already stronger than he realized.

I massaged him briskly fore and aft—head, spine, base of tail—the way I knew he liked. He had a good-size head, broad across the forehead, and perfectly shaped ears that were set rather low. His tail, a thick rope without any feathering, rode high off his spine, which Dad said indicated he'd be a great runner in the field if he could ever be trained out of his shyness. His eyes were a deep brown color, almost black, and the expression in them was mild.

"C'mon, dude," I said as we headed for the grassy practice yard, which lay parallel to the edge of the lake.

After twenty minutes I had Bingo heeling well, but he still was careless about coming around to the left side to sit. Each time he sort of caved over on his rear end and leaned into my knee, as if sitting up straight took too much energy. Any judge would mark him down for sloppiness if he behaved like that in the ring. We did a couple rounds of sit, stay, and come, plus some gaiting, which Bingo thought was a game. Then I fished in my jeans for a biscuit. Dad liked to use rewards to reinforce a training session.

"Okay, Bingo," I said, excusing him from class, "that's enough for today." Tomorrow maybe he'd sit up better. I kept the lead on his collar and when I turned to face the lake, Bingo did too.

Would you believe he's water shy? Dad had said. Though we weren't training him to retrieve, I knew Dad worried it might be an indication of Bingo's overall personality. I looked down at the top of Bingo's sleek black head. He must have felt my eyes on him because he looked up with his sweet, dark eyes.

But what if Dad was mistaken?

What would happen if *I* took Bingo down to the water's edge? Maybe when Dad tried him in water Bingo still felt new and strange at Brookfield. It was possible he wasn't actually afraid; maybe he'd just had a bad day. I imagined the big smile that would cross Dad's face when I told him, *Guess what? Bingo doesn't have a problem after all!*

Holding the lead lightly, I trotted toward the water's edge. Bingo loped cheerfully at my side as if we were were going to do nothing more serious than play some kind of game.

When we got to the water I went right up to the edge, but Bingo held back. I reached down to flick a few drops of water in his direction. He flinched like a little kid who'd just been introduced to his first wading pool.

"Hey, Bingo, if Colonel Wortham ever decides to hunt with you, this stuff's going to be important," I coaxed. "C'mon, it isn't even cold." Sometimes, the chill of the water can put a dog off and make him reluctant to get so much as a toenail wet.

Bingo inched closer to the water, stiff legged, his head held straight out like a pumpkin on a stick. He sniffed suspiciously, then lowered his muzzle to take a drink. I had my old beat-up sneakers on, so I stepped into the water halfway up to my knees. Bingo pulled back again, not hard, but insistently. He rolled his eyes back till they looked like white half-moons in his black face.

"Listen, it's okay, Bingo," I soothed, massaging his head again. I didn't let on that I was disappointed. "Don't worry. Some of us are slow starters." I should know. Bingo was like me. Like Jason Conrad. "Anyway, I still love you."

I still love you . . .

Those were words nobody at Brookfield was ever supposed to say. They went against another one of Dad's rules. *It's a big mistake to get too emotionally attached to a dog that doesn't really belong to you,* he'd warned the whole family more than once. I couldn't help myself, though. There was something about Bingo I'd loved right from the beginning. I think it was because Bingo was like me. Quiet. Shy. A little backward.

As we headed back for the kennel, I thought about Bingo's hang-up. Although it was rare, sometimes a Lab—usually a confident breed—could have a funny streak like Bingo did. Dad said some of them could be trained out of it; some never could. Which kind would Bingo turn out to be?

When Bingo and I got back to his kennel I opened the gate, pointed, and gave a firm voice command. "In! In!" He ducked into it as neat as you please. Later, when we took him to a show, he'd understand the word so well it'd be easy to get him to return to a carrier after he'd done his work in the ring.

I'd just closed the gate to his pen and was headed to pick up Chessie when I heard the racket at the other end of the shed. I turned. I couldn't believe what I saw.

An unfamiliar, lean, liver-colored dog that looked

like it could be part Doberman was circling Michael and Joey, its hackles raised up as stiff as the roach on the spine of a wild pig, the kind you see in jungle movies. Its lips were peeled back from its narrow muzzle, showing gleaming rows of sharp white teeth. Its ears were laid flat to its skull.

Joey stood there, paralyzed. His new suntan was bleached as white as a clean T-shirt. Michael was frozen too. He held onto his broom as though he couldn't remember what he'd just been using it for.

About the last thing a professional kennel keeper wants is an unexpected mating, but sometimes male dogs from the neighborhood come skulking around Brookfield, attracted by the scent of one of our female boarders who's come in heat. It usually didn't take much to scare them off. Once, though, Dad had to load a shotgun with salt pellets and blast away at Pete, Mr. Gregory's St. Bernard.

Dogs can always tell when a person's scared, and it was plain this one had Joey's number. When he feinted in Joey's direction, my brother let out a shriek and ran toward Michael. But the minute Joey moved, the dog feinted again. This time its teeth grazed Joey's bare leg just enough to leave two long red scratches behind his knee.

Then the intruder squared off at Michael. I saw Michael raise his broom and figured he intended to take a whack at the mutt. But he lifted the broom level with his chest and held it horizontally, one hand on each end. When the dog lunged again, Michael lunged forward at exactly the same moment. He forced the broom between the dog's open jaws, then pressed him backward against the fence.

Surprised, the dog yelped and sidled off. Still not

convinced, it made a second pass at Michael. One more time Michael lifted the broom handle horizontally and forced it between the mutt's jaws, pressing him backward again so hard the mutt lost its balance and rolled sideways. It scrambled to its feet, tucked its snip of a tail close to its rear end, and skedaddled down the driveway toward the county road. It must've decided taking a third chance on romance wasn't worth it.

Joey slumped back against the fence of run number 1. "Where'd you learn how to do that?" he croaked, his color coming back.

Michael laughed. "I took a jousting class once."

"Jousting?" Joey echoed with a frown.

"That's what knights in merry old England used to do—have jousting contests with each other." He looked at me as if I ought to understand exactly what he was talking about. I didn't have a clue.

"In King Arthur's time, men used a stout piece of oak about the length of this broom handle to protect themselves while fighting," he explained. "A while ago I wanted to find out more about how people really lived back in those days—ergo, when my folks took us to England on vacation I signed up for a jousting class."

"Ergo?" Joey repeated, his eyes squinty. I smiled because *I* knew what it meant.

"It means 'therefore,'" Michael said. Mrs. Graham would've put a star beside his name.

Michael's eyes were so blue and merry it was impossible to believe anything bad had ever happened to him. Joey walked up and hugged him around the waist. If I'd been a little kid Joey's age, I would've done exactly the same thing. Michael was better than brave. He could joust and use a word like "ergo" too. Best of all, he'd mentioned when his folks took *us* to England. He'd mentioned Matthew, sort of, and it hadn't made him look sad at all.

After supper, when Michael and Kim went for their usual walk around the lake and Mom and I were the only ones in the kitchen, I told her about the jousting class and how Michael knew what "ergo" meant.

"You were right about me liking him better after we worked together awhile," I told her. Which was true, but it wasn't the whole truth. Part of the reason I felt different about Michael now was because I knew about what happened to Matthew.

Kim hadn't actually made me promise not to tell about the accident. I was glad she hadn't, because it's hard to keep big stuff like that to yourself. So I said, "Mom, did Kim tell you about—" Then I stopped myself before I went any further.

"Um?" she said as she wiped off the counter. I sat down at the table, because telling what I knew seemed sort of treacherous and made my knees wobbly.

"Mom, did Kim tell you about Michael's brother?" I spit it out before I had time to think about it.

She sat down across from me. "Yes, she did, Sarah." My mother sighed and moved the dishcloth in circles as if trying to wipe a stubborn bit of grunge off the table. "It was such an unfortunate thing, but from what I've observed Michael seems to be dealing with it very well."

"Does Dad know about it too?"

"Kim told us at the same time, Sarah. We've talked about it since she did, and your dad feels pretty much the way I do. You know, that it must've been a terrible loss but that Michael's handling things fine."

Whew. What a relief. It had been hard to haul what I knew around day after day.

"What about Joey?" I asked.

"Well, we thought Joey might be a little too young to fully understand it. We haven't said anything to him yet. It seems that Kim is very serious about Michael, so there'll be lots of time to explain it to him later."

Which was okay with me. Joey was only eight; he'd be going into third grade next year. I got up and gave my mother a hug.

"What was that for?" she asked, pleased.

"Once, somebody told me I was lucky. I think maybe I am," I said.

chapter eight

On Saturday Kim and Michael and Joey and I were having a snack when Kim's best friend from high school, Melinda Willey, called and asked if she wanted to come to a party at the Round House. It's a place on the edge of Meadowville, where my sister and all her old buds used to hang out.

"You don't need to ask me twice!" Kim whooped, without even asking Michael if he wanted to go too. When she laid the news on him, he seemed a little startled. Which surprised me, considering he'd probably gone to lots of parties at college. To hear Kim talk you'd think going to St. Alban's was just one big blast, so I was surprised when she got her name on the dean's list every quarter.

"So far I've only met a few of your Meadowville friends," Michael said slowly. I wondered if he thought they'd be lots different from the ones Kim had at St. Alban's. "I'll feel sort of like a fish out of water."

"Not to fret, dear boy," Kim answered as airily as you please. "These guys are so easy to get acquainted with you'll think you've known 'em forever." She gave his shoulder a squeeze as she passed behind his chair on the way to get some mayonnaise out of the fridge.

"But if you don't want to go, I'll just tootle off by myself," she added just as airily.

Michael looked even more shocked. "At St. Alban's it was mostly just you and me doing stuff, just the two of us," he said. His voice had a frayed, anxious sound. "We didn't need a bunch of people around to have a good time. Did we?"

"But these guys are all my old buds," Kim said, as if that answered his question. "Melinda's going to the University of Colorado," she explained, "and Jeff and Denny Brown—they're twins and everybody calls them the Terrific Twosome—are home from Texas A & M, where they've both got football scholarships. Avis Anderson goes to State, and you'll have lots to talk about with her, Michael. She's a lit major, just like you."

Michael didn't look convinced. He glanced at me with that quirky smile that was getting to be as familiar as Dad's crooked one. "What do you think, Sarah? Should I take my chances with this wild Wisconsin bunch?"

"Absolutely," I said. "Kim's right. They're all nice and not really wild at all. Avis's sister is a year ahead of me, though, and she is, sort of."

"What's so wild about Becky Anderson?" Kim wanted to know, suddenly all ears. She plunked a fresh jar of peanut butter on the table, then got some bread and cheese.

"She's stuck on herself," I said. "I hate that. Becky thinks she's better than practically any girl in Meadowville Middle School. She's always bragging about how many guys call her up every night."

"The only reason you think that qualifies as wild is

because you're so shy yourself," Kim said matter-of-factly.

"I'm *not* shy," I objected. I didn't need Miss Congeniality explaining what was wrong with me. "In case you don't know it, Kimmy dear, there's a difference between being quiet and being shy."

It's true too, if you stop to think about it. Just because a person keeps to herself it doesn't mean she's shy. It only means she keeps to herself.

It was Mom who'd explained to me there was a difference. She told me I was a private person. I liked the way that sounded a lot better than shy, which seems to mean you're somebody with no gumption.

I've got gumption to burn. How about the time I socked Brian Ellis when he started tormenting that cat someone found in the stairwell at school? I gave him a black eye and got two hours of detention. I had to serve it in fifteen-minute sessions every afternoon after school on a bench outside Mr. Bateman's office. So did Brian. Afterward, we had to go to a class in conflict resolution.

Michael was probably like me. Like Jason Conrad. Just private, not shy. That's why he felt he'd be out of place in a roomful of Kim's old cronies who'd known each other since forever. The idea that Michael and I had privateness in common made me like him better than ever.

Just as we finished our snack, Joey heard the mailman go by and ran down to the county road. When he came back he plunked the magazines and letters and advertisements on the counter. He slid a postcard across the table at me, which meant it had to skate through a blob of mayonnaise.

"Wow! Guess who finally got some mail," he chortled.

I wiped the mayo off the card with a paper napkin

and looked at the handwriting. Maybe it was from Katie, who'd gone to visit her grandmother in Montana. But it wasn't Katie's loopy handwriting with little hearts for dots over the *i*'s. It was squinchy, pinched handwriting that I had to lean close to read, especially the part that got blurred by mayo.

"'Hi, Sarah. Disney World was kind of fun, especially visiting Epcot Center, where there's a 3-D show that makes it seem like they can shrink people. We went to Sea World too and saw Shamu, the killer whale, who looked cheerful and not much like a killer at all. Sincerely, your friend, Jason Conrad.'"

Your friend. That's exactly how a person who didn't know hot from cold would sign a postcard. Not "Having a wonderful time!" or "Wish you were here!" but like a distant cousin you didn't know very well. He didn't really need to add his last name. He was the only Jason at Meadowville. It wasn't likely I'd mistake him for anyone else.

"Who's it from?" Kim asked.

"Jason Conrad," Joey answered before I could get my mouth in motion.

"Joey, it's not polite to read other people's mail," I snapped.

"Well, it's a long way back from the mailbox. I had to have something to do," he said, not a bit apologetic.

"Back to the subject of the party at the Round House," Kim said, picking up where she'd left off. "It won't be fancy, Michael, and I really want you to go. Besides, I'm tired of walking around the lake every night, just you and me alone," she said pointedly. "This will be a perfect time for you to meet lots of the Meadowville guys. You'll like 'em—and Avis will talk your ear off about books."

Michael threw up his hands in pretend surrender. "Okay, okay! Just don't make me feel like somebody's prize pig."

Kim leaned against him and nuzzled his cheek. "And this little piggy went to a party," she teased, tweaking his nose.

That's how my sister is. It doesn't make her uncomfortable to shower people with attention or tease them. In a way, I sort of envied that. Would I ever be able to nuzzle Jason Conrad and think of a nursery rhyme to whisper in his ear while I grabbed him by the beak? Just thinking about it made my armpits sticky.

When Dad came in from the kennel shed, Joey handed him his mail, which he opened with one of the peanut butter knives after wiping it clean on Kim's napkin. "Here's some good news," he announced. "The sanctioned show that got canceled because of the storm two weeks ago has been rescheduled for next weekend at the fairgrounds in Milwaukee."

He braced a fist on his hip and squinted thoughtfully through the window above the sink. "Maybe I can still get a couple of Brookfield dogs down there like I'd wanted and see if they can pick up a few points."

"Which dogs?" I asked, sitting up straighter. "Bingo, maybe?" I crossed my fingers and said a prayer it would be yes.

"No way, Sarah. Bingo's a country mile away from being ready to go public. He's still too self-conscious to be put into a showring. But that Gordon setter might be ready, not to mention that sassy little Roman Candle who's beginning to look so sharp."

"Can I go with you?" I asked.

"If you get to, I do too!" Joey piped up.

Dad folded up the letter. "We can talk about that

later, guys. Tomorrow you and I will put several of the pooches through their paces, Sarah. We'll figure out which ones would be most apt to do well."

Kim, of course, couldn't care less about which dog went to what show. The only thing on her mind was the Round House. She hopped up from the table and headed for the stairs.

"Well, I've gotta wash my hair and figure out what to wear tonight," she called back merrily. Her hair looked fine to me. And she'd just told Michael it wasn't going to be fancy, so how come she had to pick out something special to wear?

Michael sighed and watched her gallop up the stairs. "While she's doing that, do you want to play a game of chess, Joey?" It was plain he still wasn't thrilled about meeting her old buds. Even Avis.

For a while I watched Joey and Michael play chess, which was as exciting as watching paint dry. Upstairs, I heard Kim turn on the shower. Everyone had something to do. Me? I scraped the plates, stuck them in the dishwasher, and put the mayo back in the fridge. I felt like a drudge. All I needed were six white mice, a pumpkin, and a fairy godmother. Plus a prince who didn't think killer whales looked like killers.

I followed Dad out to the kennel shed. A Gordon setter is about the same size as a Lab but has a long, silky black coat accented with distinct mahogany-colored markings on its chest and flanks. The Gordon Dad was talking about reminded me of a philosophy professor. He was polite, and his eyes—dark brown and set medium deep in his skull—were wise, as if he knew a lot of stuff he wasn't telling anyone. Dad called him Web, but his registered name was Daniel Webster's Pride and Joy, because it was Daniel Webster, the one we read about in sixth-grade history, who was the first person to import Gordons to America from Scotland.

"This fellow has turned out to be one of the nicest guys I ever worked with in a long while," Dad said as he took Web out of his run, slipped a collar on him, and clipped a lead to it.

"You said Bingo was nice too," I reminded him. I hated for Bingo to have to take a backseat to other dogs, even to Web.

"Sure did," he admitted with a big grin. "I'm sure you remember how I felt when Bingo first got here, I took one look at his great conformation, that super coat, those straight legs, and said to myself, 'Here's a winner!'"

Then Dad's grin faded. "But, Sarah, I get this feeling in my gut I'll never be able to train him out of that shy streak. Sometimes you can't, no matter what kind of a trainer you are. The plain truth is Bingo might never make it to Westminster. In fact, I'm wondering if we might end up having to return the fee that Colonel Wortham paid us up front."

It made me queasy when Dad talked about money. In our family there never seemed to be quite enough, so I was relieved when he handed Web's lead to me and didn't say any more about Colonel Wortham's fee. Web's lead, a long leather thong, was about the same color he was, and in a showring wouldn't draw attention away from the dog himself.

"You have a go with him, Sarah," Dad invited.

I put Web through his paces almost perfectly. He was a long-legged dog with a loose stride, and I matched mine to his so that he moved freely and easily, just like I'd watched Dad do.

"I'll go get little Dandy Randy, Sarah, and work with you," Dad said after I'd gaited Web back and forth a few minutes. "It'll be good for both Web and the terrier. It's important for each of 'em to learn not to be rattled by the presence of another dog in the ring," he explained.

So we worked together, passing each other going back and forth, correcting our dogs each time they craned their heads around to see what the other one was doing.

Of course, it was Dad who'd be doing the showing in Milwaukee, but in my mind's eye it was me who was in the ring. The youngest person there. Wearing a tan outfit that wouldn't distract the judges' attention from Web's black and mahogany looks. The crowd applauded as we did our routine. When the scores were added up, I'd won first place. Flashbulbs popped; the press crowded around. *In your dreams, Sarah!*

When we were finished, Dad had some tips for me. "For the day when you eventually get in the ring," he said with a wink. "Now, with a dark dog like Web here, you want to make sure you position him under the lights, if possible. That's because a dark-coated dog can almost disappear in the gloom of some of these old show barns." Then he took the lead and showed me something else.

"I'm going to put Web through his paces again, Sarah, but notice I handle him as little as possible. The less he's managed, the more alert and in control of himself he'll seem to be from the judges' viewpoint. Watch now—"

Dad took off around the outside edge of our mini-arena while I held Dandy Randy aside. He's light on his feet—Dad, I mean—and sure enough, Web looked like he was doing everything without any help from his handler—gaiting, pausing, sitting, even stacking.

I glanced back at the kennels. I could see Bingo waiting patiently at the door of his run. Even though I didn't want to, I started thinking about shyness again. Mine. Bingo's. Michael's. We were alike, the three of us, and in a way we all were trying to be something else.

When I changed my name to Darla would it really make me different than I was?

Could I say something to Michael that'd help him have a good time at the Round House?

If I worked extra hard with Bingo could I bring him up to speed?

Questions I didn't have answers for.

But when we were through for the day I asked Dad the same question I'd asked him in the kitchen, because I knew it was the kind that did have an answer. "So, if you decide for sure to go to Milwaukee, do you think I could come with you?"

He laid his arm across my shoulders. "Yep, I think you should, Sarah. You're really doing well, and it's time you got some professional exposure. Not that you'll be showing—I'll do that—but I can teach you how to scope out a showring, how to get registered, how to size up the judges, all that insider stuff." He gave me a squeeze with one hand while smoothing the top of Web's head with the other, and gave me a crooked grin.

"I think you're gonna be like your old man, Sarah. Your life's gonna go to the dogs, just like mine did."

It's neat to have a dad who talks to you like that. It means being shy doesn't count. It made me feel closer to him than ever. So close that I mentioned what Kim had told me about Matthew.

Dad sighed the same way Mom had and wagged his head. "It's just a darn shame, Sarah."

"Do people ever get over things like that?" I asked.

Dad didn't answer right away. "They can, but it takes a long time," he said slowly. "Even then, some small reminder can bring the grief back in a way that makes everything seem as fresh and painful as if it'd happened yesterday."

"I'm glad Kim brought him home for the summer," I said. Words I never thought would ever come out of my mouth. "He can just be himself here because we're all so ordinary."

My dad faked a crestfallen look. "I beg your pardon! I've always thought we Connellys were quite *extra*ordinary," he said. "Not run-of-the-mill at all!"

I knew what he meant. We were. But the neat thing was, Dad knew what *I* meant.

chapter nine

"If we're going to Milwaukee on Friday, I'd better change that leaky left rear tire on the van. No sense waiting till the last minute," Dad said on Tuesday morning when we all went out to start the day's work. He arched his back as if there was a tender spot on his spine, clamped his cap firmly on his head, and headed off to the garage.

"You kids go ahead and get started," he called over his shoulder. "I'll catch up with you later."

Besides me moving into Kim's room, there was one other thing that made the summer different from any other. Nobody had to nag Joey to do his share anymore. He was so crazy to be with Michael that he did everything but cartwheels the minute it was time to go to work.

Which shouldn't have been any skin off my nose. Except it was, a little. Sometimes I felt more jealous of Joey than I did of Kim. He and Michael were together practically all the time, just the two of them, cleaning kennels, fishing, playing chess, or just plain hanging out. I sort of wished it was me.

I had just taken Web out of his kennel when I heard Dad give a loud, sharp cry. I turned to see Joey and Michael staring toward the garage. Michael started to run before I did, but it was Joey, being small and as quick as a flea, who got there first. He let out a shriek you could've heard all the way down in Meadowville.

We found Dad lying on the garage floor, the left rear end of the van slumped over on its axle. He'd put the van up on a jack and had gotten the tire off, then the jack must've started to slip. He'd probably lunged forward— even though his back was feeling tender—and strained against the side of the van, hoping to keep it from slipping off all the way. His face was white, his lips pulled back from his teeth in a snarl of pain, like the raccoon we caught in a trap once. There was another expression in his eyes I couldn't quite read.

Michael knelt swiftly at his side. "What happened, Mr. Connelly?" His voice was calm. If he was scared, it didn't show.

"I think . . . I might've slipped a disk," my dad groaned. "Did it once before . . . when I tried out for . . . varsity pole vaulting." He squeezed the words between his teeth while beads of sweat as big as raindrops popped out on his forehead.

"Stay still," Michael said, as cool as a cucumber. He turned to Joey and me. "Is there a hospital in Meadowville with an emergency room?"

"Yep," Joey answered before I could. He took his cue from Michael and was calm now too. No tears at all, even though Dad was still wearing his raccoon snarl. "I had to go there last summer when I snagged my big toe with a fishhook."

"Does it have an ambulance service?"

"No," I said, before Joey beat me to it. "There's a volunteer service, but it'll take 'em a while to get here."

"I b-b-better go g-g-get Mom," Joey stammered. The whole thing was suddenly too much for him, and there was a familiar quiver in my brother's voice.

"She went down to Mrs. Anderson's for a meeting of the Sew Bees quilt club," I reminded him.

"Then we'll have to take your dad in ourselves," Michael said. "First, we need to get something stiff under him—a board, maybe. Then we'll have to get him into the back of the pickup because we can't take time to fix the tire on the van. Can you think of anything we can use?"

"There's a big piece of plywood behind the garage," Joey announced. "We were going to cut it up to make bluebird houses."

"That oughta work . . . just fine," Dad croaked. "My hospital policy doesn't cover . . . ambulance service any-way." I looked down at him. Lying there, white and sweaty and grim, all he could think of was what it might cost for an ambulance.

"I'll get it," I said, and flew outside to where the ply-wood was propped against the side of the garage, covered with a sheet of plastic to keep the rain off. The plastic was taped on so I just grabbed everything and dashed back inside.

"Perfect!" Michael exclaimed when he saw the plas-tic. "It's slick, which'll make it easier for us to pull your dad across it into the middle of the board."

"How come we have to do that?" Joey wanted to know as Michael laid the plywood on the garage floor next to Dad.

"Because we don't know exactly what's wrong with your dad's back. If he did more than slip a disk—like if he broke something—we shouldn't move him any more'n we have to. To be on the safe side, we gotta keep his spine stable, and not flex him one way or the other."

Michael got down on the floor, put his arms around my dad's shoulders, and began to inch him carefully onto the plastic-covered plywood. I helped by hooking my fingers in Dad's belt loops and tugging him along. Joey took the cuffs of Dad's jeans and moved his legs, slowly, slowly. All the while Dad kept his eyes squinched shut and his teeth bared.

"Now what?" I asked when we got him into the middle of the plywood. "How do we lift him up, board and all, into the pickup so we can get him into town?"

"Good question," Michael admitted, nibbling his lip.

"Go down the road . . . get Buck Gregory," Dad whispered. "He can help . . . the man's as strong as an ox . . . "

"You're fast on your feet, Joey," Michael said. "Can you go get Mr. Gregory?" Joey charged out of the garage like he'd been set on fire, then Michael turned to me. "Why don't you get a cold glass of water for your dad, Sarah."

"A couple aspirin too," Dad whispered.

"While you're doing that, I'll back up the truck so we don't have to haul your dad very far once Mr. Gregory gets here," he said as we headed out of the garage together.

When Mr. Gregory showed up, all two hundred fifty pounds of him, he sized up the situation. "I'll take this side and you three kids get over there," he instructed. "On the count of three we'll hoist together and slide 'im right into the bed of the truck."

"Sounds . . . good . . . to me," Dad said. The collar of his green shirt was dark with perspiration, and his whole face was covered with raindrops of sweat.

"One . . . two . . . three!" Mr. Gregory bellowed, and

we all hoisted like crazy. There wasn't much Joey could really do, being only eight, but Michael was a lot stronger than he looked. We had Dad all the way into the back of the truck by the count of four. Then I hopped into the truck bed myself and gave Dad the glass of water and the aspirin.

"Who's going to show me the way to the hospital?" Michael asked, looking first at me and then at Joey.

"Joey better do it, Michael," I said, sorry I couldn't be the one. "Since Mom's gone, I better stay here to make sure the dogs are okay."

Mr. Gregory and I watched the truck move slowly down the drive, turn at the mailbox, then move smoothly east toward town, four miles away.

Just before Mr. Gregory started down the drive himself he turned to me with a quizzical look. "That boy you called Michael did some quick thinking by not manhandling Dan any more than necessary," he said. Then he grinned. "Must be one of Kimmy's new boyfriends, huh?"

I nodded and wiped my sweaty hands on the seat of my shorts. "They're going to get married," I said. I didn't want him to think Michael was just another guy, not like all the other ones she'd dragged home.

They're going to get married. I was beginning to like the way the words sounded.

Mr. Gregory bobbed his head as if he approved. "I think your sister picked a winner this time," he said.

"I gave him my room for the summer," I told him, making it sound as if I'd done it voluntarily. Mr. Gregory waved one of his bear paws at me as he climbed into his own truck. "Well, I'd say young Michael is pretty lucky to get in with you Connellys."

I would've told Mr. Gregory that's exactly what Michael thought too, but he drove off before I had a chance. I was sorry to see him go. It was sort of lonely when there weren't any more heroics to be part of. But what if Dad did something worse than slip a disk? I tried to put the picture of him lying there on the garage floor out of my mind.

I thought of calling Mom at Mrs. Anderson's, then decided to wait. Dad might have to stay at the hospital overnight, maybe even longer. Since Michael and Joey had only gotten two pens cleaned, the others had to be finished. I needed something to do, so I picked up where they'd left off. Working would (a) get the job done and (b) keep me from thinking too much about what Dad's accident actually meant.

Because it meant for sure we wouldn't be going to Milwaukee. Web wouldn't have a chance to earn any points; Dandy Randy would have to wait till another time too.

It's a funny thing about doing work you know how to do: Because you don't actually have to figure out what to do next, you've got plenty of time to just plain t-h-i-n-k.

Would you believe by the time I'd finished scooping poop and hosing down the runs, I had an idea? Maybe there was a way we could go to Milwaukee after all.

Everyone got home just before supper. Mom said she wished I'd called her right away, but I explained we were all kind of rattled. Dad had been x-rayed to make sure nothing was broken, and given some stuff to read about how to avoid disk injuries, plus medicine with a name you couldn't pronounce that was even better than aspirin to help his muscles relax.

Now that Dad's eyes weren't cloudy with pain, I could read the look that puzzled me earlier. He knew the same thing I did: Missing the show on Saturday was a real downer.

After Mom got Dad settled flat on his back on the couch in the living room with a heating pad and ice packs to be used alternately, and everyone else had gone off to do something else, I got a chair and sat down beside him.

"Dad, about that show in Milwaukee—"

"Well, Sarah, we'll just have to miss it, that's all," he said gruffly in the tone of voice he hardly ever uses except when he's totally bummed out.

"It's not the end of the world. It just means a couple of the dogs will fall behind schedule a little," he went on. "I'll pencil in some extra shows and we'll try to make up the points later this summer." Except Dad knew, just like I did, that moving a dog along on a fast track meant he could contract to take a new one in its place. Show dogs in training meant money in the bank; the regular boarders barely paid expenses.

"About Milwaukee, Dad," I said, handing him an ice pack and turning off the heating pad. "What I was thinking was, well, why can't I show Web and Randy?"

Dad looked straight at me and didn't say anything for a minute. Then he wagged his head.

"Real life isn't a movie script, Sarah," he warned me. "You aren't ready for the big time any more than Bingo is. It'd be different if I could be there with you, to coach you through it. But I'm pretty sure I won't feel up to making the trip by Friday." His pain medication must've started to wear off, because he clenched his teeth again, bringing back his raccoon-in-a-trap expression.

I wasn't ready to give up. I outlined my plan to him, point by point.

"Michael could finish changing the tire on the van. Mom could help me get the dogs bathed and loaded in

the carriers. Joey could get all the grooming gear together. Michael could drive us to Milwaukee. If I show
the dogs and they don't do well, what's been lost?"

Dad looked at me steadily. I could almost hear the
chink-a-chink sound of his brain turning the idea over
and over, checking it for flaws.

I offered him my final sales pitch. "But if Web or
Randy comes through, they won't be as far behind the
eight ball as if they hadn't gone to Milwaukee at all,
right?"

Dad mopped the dew off his upper lip with his shirt
sleeve. He never took his eyes off mine. "Let me think on
it, Sarah. Maybe you've come up with a not so bad idea."

After supper I went out to tell Bingo why I hadn't
picked him to go to Milwaukee. I put him on a leash and
walked him along the lake after Kim and Michael took
off for their usual hike going around the other way.

"It's because real life isn't a movie script, Bingo," I explained. "Dad says you're not ready and I'm not either,
not unless he can go to Milwaukee with me." Bingo
looked up in a way that made me think he understood
what I was saying. I knelt beside him and laid my face
against his neck. Some people don't like the way dogs
smell. I do. I took a good whiff.

"But someday we'll both be ready at the same time,
Bingo." As if to answer me he thumped his ropy black
tail in the sand. *Yes, we will,* he seemed to say. *It'll be you
and me together.*

On Friday morning, after two days of hot pads,
cold packs, painkillers, and resting flat on his back,
Dad announced that we'd be going to Milwaukee
after all. He laid the plan out for everyone just as

I'd laid it out to him, but with one change.

"We can only take Web this time. Sarah—being a be-ginner—will have her hands full working with just one dog at a time." Then he added, "Mom and Kim can stay behind to look after things at Brookfield."

Mom nodded. Kim had already left for the Kwik Pik by then, but Mom said she knew Kim would agree it was the best thing to do.

Nobody was happier than Joey, but after I'd bragged myself up about how I could fill in for Dad, I realized I probably couldn't. It was too late for a change of heart, though, especially after Michael went into town to rent a wheelchair and we made room for it in the van along with Web's carrier.

Mom aired out our sleeping bags and hauled the food coolers up from the basement. Mr. Gregory came back and helped Michael change the tire on the van. Because Mom was busy making lunches, it was Joey who helped me bathe and brush Web. I trimmed Web's toenails, cleaned his ears with a soft cotton cloth, and we were on the road to Milwaukee that afternoon as shadows from the cornfields lay like swords across the highway.

Joey sat up front with Michael. Dad and I sat behind, which gave me plenty of time to see how careful Michael was about everything he did. You'd think he'd had a lot of experience driving a van, but he told me later it was the first time ever.

The show was at the state fairgrounds, and the place was half filled with vans and campers by the time we got there. A lot of competitors liked to arrive early, just like Dad did, but we were able to get ourselves a nice spot under some trees. Michael got the wheelchair out, then Dad and I went to the auditorium to get the registration taken care of.

"Dan Connelly, what happened to *you?*" exclaimed a woman at a long table where other people were getting registered. Dog show people keep running into one other on the circuit, and it was plain she and Dad knew each other pretty well.

"It's going to be hard to show a dog from a wheel-chair, my friend!" She rolled her eyes as if she wondered why he'd even bothered to pay his registration fee.

"I brought my assistant with me," Dad said. I liked that better than if he'd said *my daughter. My assistant* sounded official and businesslike. I got my armband—number 12, white numbers on a green background—and we picked out a spot toward the far end of the show barn for Web's carrier and his gear.

"It'll be quieter down here," Dad explained, "and eas-ier on everybody's nerves."

That night as we leaned against the van just before bed-time, Michael looked up at the stars. "Look, Sarah, there's the Big Dipper. And over there, that's Cassiopeia."

"Guess you must be a star watcher," I said. I could al-ways pick out the Big Dipper but not much else, unless it was those three bright stars in a row that were in Orion's belt.

Michael didn't answer right away. When he did, his voice was soft. "It's kind of comforting to look up there and realize how immense the universe is, how small we humans are. It sort of puts our earthly concerns into per-spective."

Earthly concerns. I knew he must be thinking of what'd happened to his brother. In the dark I moved a little closer to Michael. Not so we actually touched, just till I could feel the warmth radiating from his arm

against mine. He'd gotten so tan from all the time he and
Joey spent fishing that it seemed the sun had stored its
heat in his skin.

"Michael, Kim told me," I said.

"Told you? About what?"

"You know. About Matthew." I hadn't intended to
tell him what I knew, but when Michael talked about the
sky putting the universe into perspective it seemed like a
good time.

Then it was Michael who moved closer. He took my
hand in his. His fingers warm, steely bands around mine.
"I'm glad she did, Sarah," he said. "Because you know
what? Sometimes it's nice to be able to talk to people
about it."

I wondered if I should invite him to talk about it
some more. I didn't have to, though, because he went on
in a slow, thoughtful way.

"The afternoon Matthew and I went out to target
practice seemed like any other nice summer day. Which
makes it so odd to remember now. You know, that
Matthew's last day in this world was sunny and ordinary
and for a change we weren't arguing about something."

"Did you? Argue, I mean?" I wasn't sure if I
should've asked a question like that. "Because sometimes
Kim and I argue too," I added quickly. "About stuff that
doesn't even matter. Me and Joey do too. Maybe that's
just how it is with brothers and sisters."

"It wasn't that Matthew and I didn't like each other,"
Michael went on. "We did. But Matthew was older than
me and never let me forget it." He laughed softly. "I was
always trying to catch up to him. Only I never could and
now I never can." He paused.

"Matthew being older might be one of the reasons my

folks took his loss even harder. I mean, maybe a first child is always special. What do *you* think, Sarah?"

"I think my mom and dad love Kim and Joey and me the same," I said. The minute I said it I knew it was true, so I was glad he'd asked.

But I'm not sure Michael heard me. "Sometimes, I wake up at night and the first thing I think is if I'd never come along my parents would still have Matthew," he said. "He was their golden boy. The one who was so smart. The one who was going to be a doctor, just like my father."

Inside the van I knew Dad was stretched out in a sleeping bag on the floor, the best place for somebody with a bad back. Joey had turned on the radio but kept it low. The sound of a guitar floated past our ears.

I was glad to have Michael all to myself, even if he was talking about sad stuff. It was one of those times when a person wants to say something important, something that matters.

"I know this kid who had a heart attack playing basketball and was dead before they could haul him off the court," I said, because I couldn't think of anything else. It was the only story I knew about somebody dying young and not having a chance to live till he was an old person. I repeated it, just like I'd told it to Kim.

"That's different, Sarah," Michael said.

"How's it different?" I wondered out loud. "I mean, Eddie Ripley's brother was as alive as anybody one minute, then as dead as Matthew the next, wasn't he?"

"Nobody *killed* Eddie Ripley's brother," Michael said so quietly I had to strain to hear him. "The way Eddie Ripley's brother died, how could anyone blame someone else? But with Matthew . . ." His words trailed off into silence.

I wondered if he was crying, but when Michael spoke again, there was a new note in his voice. It was as if he'd put all his painful memories in a box and turned a key, locking them inside so he wouldn't have to think about them for a while.

"Listen, enough of that," he said. He squeezed my fingers again, then dropped his voice to a conspiratorial whisper. "Sarah, I've been meaning to ask you to help me do something before we go back to Brookfield."

"Like what?" The way he said, *Sarah, I've been meaning to ask you to help me* made me feel so special that my heart bloomed like a sunflower in my chest. I would've helped him rob a bank if he'd asked me.

"I want to buy Kim a promise ring."

"A promise ring?"

"That's the kind of a ring you give a girl before you get formally engaged. A little ring before the big ring, you could say. Sometimes, I think Kim doesn't realize how much she means to me, and I want her to know. So—depending on how your dad's feeling when the show's over—d'you think you could ask him to let us stop somewhere in Milwaukee so I could buy one before we head home?"

I studied Michael's profile in the falling dark. It seemed kind of funny he wanted me to do the asking. "It's okay if you ask him yourself, Michael. You oughta know by now my dad doesn't bite. He's about as mean as Bingo!"

Michael laughed and gave my hand an extra squeeze. "Oh, I know that, Sarah. But I feel kind of funny, especially when it's something like this. I just thought it'd be easier if you did."

It was my turn to squeeze his hand. "No problem, Michael." And I knew it wouldn't be, especially if Dad's back was feeling okay. I could see Michael and me side by side in a store in Milwaukee, looking at rings, me telling him which one Kim would like best. Being sure he picked just the right one would make me more than a kid sister. I'd be part of their romance forever and ever.

chapter ten

Right from the get go, that old Daniel Webster knew why he'd come to Milwaukee. He was solemn, but he was a showman too. He had a sixth sense about how to make himself look good. Dad always said it was a big mistake to show a dog before he was at his best, and Web was proof of that. He was ready to be on stage. Bingo wasn't. Bingo might never be.

And what about me? I asked myself as we headed toward the show barn. But there was no time to worry about that. I put Web on a lead and carried the box of grooming tools under my arm, while Dad rolled along beside us in his wheelchair.

When we got set up at our bench, I brushed Web with long, steady strokes, not pulling hard, yet making sure none of his silky coat was snarly or matted. Even though I'd bathed him the day before, I checked the flesh and hair around his mouth to make sure they were clean. I wiped the corners of his eyes one last time. I made sure his ears were spotless.

"The perfect show dog has yet to be born," Dad told me as he demonstrated how to pluck a few stray black

hairs out of the mahogany-colored bib that covered
Web's chest.

"Even the winningest dog has its faults, Sarah. A
handler's job is to make sure that the dog he or she's
working with is seen to the best advantage. Minimize any
faults, enhance all the strong points—that's the secret of
a show dog's success—and the handler's too."

Dad pointed out one of Web's faults: His neck wasn't
quite as long and lean as would have been ideal. "So
when you stack him, Sarah, it'll be important to stretch
'im out. Get his head up so that shorter-than-perfect neck
will seem longer than it really is."

Without getting out of his chair, Dad reached forward to show me how. "Show dogs are just like movie
stars," he said, elevating Web's head by placing his left
hand under the dog's jaw. "They've got to have their best
side to the camera—and here in Milwaukee, the camera
will be the judges' eyes."

After I put the finishing touches on Web's grooming—I even gave his teeth a final brushing—I loosened
him up by gaiting him back and forth outside the show
barn so he could work all the kinks out of his bones.
Traveling for five hours in a carrier yesterday had made
him stiff, and he needed to get the elastic back in his step.
A handler also has to be sure a pooch has a last chance to
heed nature's call, so I made sure Web took care of that
too. There's nothing more embarrassing than a dog that
stops to lift its leg or squats to drop a few chocolates in a
showring.

I left Dad in charge of Web, then went back to the
camper to change into the outfit Mom helped me put together. Pants the color of vanilla ice cream and a cotton
shirt to match. Not a bright color, but one that would

contrast with Web's dark good looks and show him off to the best advantage. I had a new pair of Nikes so I wouldn't slip in the ring on one of the sharp turns. No jewelry, though. No fancy hair clips, no decorations except the green armband with the number 12 printed on it to guarantee the judges knew exactly which entry I was.

It wasn't hard to tell which contestants were amateurs handling their own dogs. Some were dressed up as if they were going to a party. A lady with blue hair wore a rhinestone necklace that looked like real diamonds. A man in flashy cowboy clothes had a big silver belt buckle that would've sunk him to the bottom of Echo Lake if he ever fell over the side of the *Guinevere*. Didn't they know the dog was supposed to be the star?

Michael and Joey met me when I was halfway back to the show barn and we all walked together. Michael bent down close and whispered, "You haven't forgotten what I asked you last night, have you, Sarah?"

"Like I could!" I exclaimed. Helping him pick out a promise ring for Kim was almost as important as getting points for Web. "And now you can do something for me," I said, which made his eyes widen with surprise.

"We'll leave Dad in charge of Web for a minute while we scope out the ring, okay? I can't take Web himself in till our number's called, but you 'n' me can pace it off so I can get a feel for it."

We walked the ring lengthwise, then widthwise. I checked the lighting. There were three skylights high overhead, so there wouldn't be any dark shadows for Web to get lost in.

"How d'you think it looks, Sarah?" Dad asked when

Michael and I were finished. I pointed up at the sky-lights; he nodded and grinned.

Then a voice over the loudspeaker called for the first contestants, the nonsporting class. I felt sweaty and wished I hadn't eaten breakfast because it began to flop around in my stomach like a load of wet towels in a dryer. Then it was the turn of the hunter-retriever class to show. A yellow Lab handled by a man about Dad's age went up first. Next came a woman with a German short-hair retriever. Third was a woman with another Gordon setter. I studied her dog with a narrow eye. I was sure Web was classier.

"Number 12, Daniel Webster's Pride and Joy, shown by Sarah Connelly," came a voice over the loudspeaker. My heart clanged against my ribs.

Dad pulled me down to his wheelchair. "Pretend you're back home in our ring at Brookfield," he said. "Stay calm; be relaxed. You're gonna do just fine, Sarah."

Even Joey wished me luck, and when I glanced at Michael, his blue eyes were shiny. He didn't say anything, just mouthed the words *Good luck,* and gave me two thumbs up.

I gaited Web back and forth in front of the judges' stand, and he moved beside me in his flowing silk paja-mas as if he'd been in front of an audience all his life. When the judges wanted stacking, I stacked him, mak-ing sure his head was up, and clucked softly to him so he kept his eyes trained on me. A lady judge came and in-spected Web's ears and eyes, teeth and toes, then I was waved aside while a golden retriever took the ring.

"Number 12!" came the voice over the loudspeaker again. Web and I moved up to show again, this time with only five other hunter-retrievers, the Gordie among them. I was sweatier now, and didn't dare look over at Dad or Michael or Joey.

We all went back to the sidelines, then four numbers were called out. The yellow Lab, the Gordie, the German shorthair—and number 12. The three judges looked each dog over carefully, inspecting the chest and belly of each, checking legs for soundness, assessing the set of the ears.

Tension wrapped cold iron bands around my chest. I couldn't breathe. Only three numbers were called the next time. Number 12 was one of them. That in-your-dreams scene came back to me—flashbulbs popping, TV video cameras hovering near, a blue ribbon in my hand.

Web seemed to move more confidently than ever and my sweat began to dry. The three of us—the man with the yellow Lab, the woman with the German shorthair, and me—gaited our dogs again, stacked them, gaited them again, and stood for another inspection. An official came forward with the ribbons, blue, red, and white. A moment before I hadn't been able to breathe. Now I deliberately tried not to.

The man with the yellow Lab looked expectant, as if he knew his dog would get the blue. I closed my eyes and prayed he didn't. "First place, number 9, California Gold, shown by Henry Bishop. Please step forward." I started to breathe again.

"Second place, number 12, Daniel Webster's Pride and Joy, shown by Sarah Connelly, second place." I opened my eyes. I even managed to step forward. No flashbulbs popped, but I heard the whir of a video camera behind me. The woman with the German shorthair got third.

"You did it!" Joey squealed. "You got a red ribbon!"

"Great job, Sarah!" Dad said, and struggled out of his wheelchair long enough to give me a bear hug.

Michael reached out and wrapped me up in his long, thin, brown arms. "Kim's going to be so proud of you," he whispered in my ear as he gave me a hard squeeze. What mattered most was that *he* was.

"I told Dad you wanted to stop to buy something for Kim," I said to Michael as we packed up after the show, "and he said it's okay to drive into Milwaukee." I hadn't told Dad that Michael wanted to stop at a jewelry store. I liked the idea that it was our secret, just Michael's and mine.

He flashed me a glance that was filled with so much light I had to blink. "Thanks, Sarah. You're not only a winner, you're a real princess." Sheesh! Web got a second and now I was a princess. Eventually maybe I'd get a carriage and a prince to go with the title.

"I bought a newspaper while you were getting Web ready this morning," Michael informed me as we repacked the cooler with fresh ice and cans of soda for the trip home, "and I found a shopping mall on the way out of town. There's a place there called The Jewel Box, and it'll save us the hassle of going all the way downtown."

The Jewel Box turned out to be a tiny shop tucked into a corner of the Evergreen Mall. Not only did it sell rings and bracelets and earrings, but clocks and watches and barometers too. Dad and Joey waited in the van while Michael and I looked at trays of rings after he explained to the clerk what he wanted.

"I can't buy an official engagement ring yet," he said, as if he needed to apologize.

"We sell many promise rings, sir," the clerk, a white-haired lady who looked like my aunt Ethel in Green Bay, assured him with a smile. "Many young people are in the same situation you're in. Long on love, short on cash."

There were rings with tiny stones of every color in the rainbow—red, blue, green, amethyst, topaz. Then there were plain rings without any stones but decorated with carvings of vines and roses. For some reason, I liked them best. Among them, I found the absolutely all-time perfect promise ring.

"Look at this," I whispered to Michael, and held up one that showed two hands—one gold, the other silver—clasped together. The fingers of each were crafted so carefully you could even see their tiny fingernails. The hands gripped each other as if neither intended to let the other go.

Michael studied it a moment. He grinned at me in his quirky way. "It's kind of medieval," he mused. "How appropriate. Thanks, Sarah. This is exactly what I was looking for."

The clerk put the ring in a box with a blue velvet cushion, then wrapped the box in silver paper. Michael paid for it and tucked the box into his jacket. His eyes gleamed like the blue stones in the ring tray.

"Do you think Kim will like it?" he asked as we walked across the parking lot to the van. All of a sudden, he seemed to doubt the choice he'd made. That I helped him make.

"Like it? She'll *love* it!" I exclaimed. I knew she would, because I did, even though I wasn't a romantic person, not the way Kim was.

But there was something I had to know. I asked quick, before we got to the van. "When're you going to give it to Kim? Maybe at breakfast tomorrow?"

"No, not then. I want to pick a special time. Maybe

when we're walking around Echo Lake tomorrow night, just the two of us."

I was sorry. I wanted to see my sister peel that silver paper off, open the box, and see the ring nestled there on its little blue velvet pillow. I wanted to see her cheeks get pink; I wanted to see how she looked at Michael. I wanted to be there when she squealed, "Oh, Michael! It's absolutely *per*fect!"

After we piled back into the van, I felt pooped. The long trip to Milwaukee yesterday, actually winning second place today, buying a promise ring—I'd had more excitement in two days than I'd had in my whole life. If you didn't count the time I bonked Brian Ellis and gave him a black eye.

The van was warm and I dozed off. My dreams were topsy-turvy, mostly about two hands, one gold, the other silver, clasped together as if they'd never ever let the other go. You'd think I'd have dreamed about winning my first-ever red ribbon. Instead, I dreamed about a wedding and Michael Miller being folded into the Connelly family forever.

We got home just after midnight. All the windows in the house were dark except for the living room, where Mom always left a small light on over the TV. After settling Web in his kennel, we stumbled off to our rooms. I peeled off my vanilla ice-cream pants and shirt and crawled under my sheets in my underwear.

"Is that you, Sarah?" Kim murmured sleepily.

"No, it's the famous Brookfield burglar," I said.

"How was the show?" she asked with a yawn.

"Fine." I didn't elaborate. For once, I was almost too tired to talk. I'd save everything for Sunday breakfast.

"So what'd you and Mom do while we were gone?" I

asked as I pulled up my sheet. I hoped she wouldn't go into detail.

"Um, not much," Kim answered vaguely. "Mom worked in her flower bed. We both took care of the dogs. Then I just, um, hung out."

"Hung out?" Suddenly I was alert. Hardly tired at all. "Where at? Who with?" I demanded.

"Melinda called. I met her and the gang back at the Round House."

"Again?" Why wasn't once enough? "How come? I mean, Michael wasn't even here to go with you." I raised up on one elbow. I remembered what Michael said the first day out on the lake, about how Merlin warned Arthur that Guinevere would cause him sorrow. If Kim caused Michael any sorrow, well, I'd just—

"Oh, for heaven's sake, Sarah! Don't be such an old granny," Kim snapped. Now she was as wide awake as I was. "For once I didn't have to worry whether Michael felt left out. You know how that can be."

I didn't have a clue, since I'd never gone to a party with anyone in my entire life. Some kids in my grade did, but my last one was Katie's birthday party when she was ten and her mom took a bunch of us to Chuck E. Cheese's, where Lester Pritchard got sick and barfed all over the place.

"It's not like Michael and I have to be tied together every single minute, Sarah. I'm not one of those dogs you're so crazy about. I can't be trained to sit and stay. Anyway, what do *you* know about this kinda stuff? You've never actually had a boyfriend yet."

Which was true, but it seemed spiteful of her to point it out. What I *did* know was that Michael had forgotten all about Merlin's warning and had bought a gold and silver promise ring. Maybe he was across the hall this very minute, thinking how Kim would smile and throw her arms around his neck when he gave it to her.

"So, exactly who else was at the Round House?" I asked. Somehow, it seemed to be my duty to pry into the matter on Michael's behalf. After all, it was me who'd helped him pick out the ring. I was part of their romance now. I had an investment to protect.

"Just the regular bunch. It was like old times."

"Old times?"

"Yes. When I didn't have to worry about every little thing I said or how I acted or if I was hurting somebody's feelings. I could just be me, not some kind of counselor or social worker."

"Counselor? Social worker? What're you talking about, Kim?"

For a long moment she didn't answer. "I think Michael needs more than I can give him, Sarah," she said slowly. "He's sort of like a little kid, you know?" I didn't know any such thing. Joey was a little kid; Michael wasn't.

"Michael—well, he *clings* to me, Sarah. He says he doesn't know what he'd do if he ever lost me, like I was something he found and now he's got to hang on to me, no matter what." She paused. "Sarah, remember those kittens Gram had one year at the cottage?"

Sure I remembered; one was gray, one was white, and one had stripes. "Remember how when you held them up to your shoulder they just dug their little claws in and held on for dear life?" Kim asked. I remembered that too.

"But Michael isn't a kitten," I reminded her. "It's just that he likes you a lot, Kim. Lots and lots." I wished I could tell her about the ring.

"Sometimes, lots and lots can be too much," Kim said.

Then she didn't say any more, so I didn't either. After a little while I heard her start to wuffle softly as she drifted off to sleep.

The last thing I saw before I went to sleep myself were those two tiny hands clasped together as if they'd never let go. I knew Kim would feel different as soon as she saw them. In a flash, she'd realize she loved Michael as much as he loved her. *She had to.* Otherwise, how could he be folded into the Connelly family forever and ever?

chapter eleven

"Folks, you wouldn't believe this kid," Dad told everyone at breakfast on Sunday morning. "She brought Web through with flying colors. Sarah's a credit to Brookfield Kennel, and then some."

He looked across the table at me in a way that made me feel as if I could climb cliffs if I had to. Rescue people from burning buildings. Snatch small children off railroad tracks just before the noon freight went by. No more sour Sarah. Suddenly, I was super Sarah.

Mom made dollar pancakes, my favorites, and I ate about thirteen dollars' worth slathered with homemade raspberry syrup before I quit. Dad went on regaling everyone with what a prince Web was, how I didn't overhandle him, how impressed his show buddies were with the way I'd taken over for a poor old guy with a slipped disk.

"Let me tell you, that Gordie's coat flowed around him like watered silk," Dad said. "If he keeps going this way there's not much doubt in my mind he'll make it all the way to Westminster."

Naturally I was glad that Web got so much praise,

but in the back of my mind I thought, One of these days you'll be able to say those things about Bingo too.

Mom looked pleased to hear all about it, and since Joey'd been in Milwaukee to see and hear everything firsthand, he didn't pay any attention at all. Michael didn't really listen either. His eyes were kind of dreamy, and I knew he was thinking about a certain pair of clasped hands in a box lined with blue velvet. It wasn't till I went upstairs to make up my cot that I realized there was one person at the table who hadn't said one single solitary word about my new fame.

When Kim followed me up and started on her own bed, I flashed a quick glance in her direction. My sister's one of those people who never act depressed, but there was a different look on her face as she smoothed her sheets and plumped her pillows.

The truth hit me like a blow right between the eyes. On top of what she'd told me last night about Michael being as clingy as a kitten, Miss Congeniality was jealous of her own sister!

For a split second I was happy. *She* was jealous of *me* for a change, rather than the other way around. Then I remembered how it felt to feel that way. It was as if your innards were twisted up inside. Your heart felt pinched and dried up. The face you stared at in the mirror didn't look like your own anymore. Life's not much fun when you're jealous.

"Hey, Kim. You're not mad at me are you?" I asked.

She acted surprised. "Mad at you?" I figured she was pretending. "About what, for heaven's sake?"

"You know. Me doing so great with Web. Dad bragging me up. Telling everybody how great I was. I only got second place," I reminded her. "Anyway, it's not like you ever wanted to show any of the dogs yourself. So

there's no reason for you to be bent out of shape, right?"
I didn't use the *J* word, because I remembered I didn't
like it when Mom used it on me.

Kim straightened up and swept her fingers through
her bright, curly hair. "Don't be silly, Sarah. Of course
I'm not bent out of shape. I'm glad everything went so
well for you guys in Milwaukee." She looked straight at
me. Her green eyes were clear and—although I didn't
want her to feel too tormented—I was a little disappointed to realize she was telling the truth.

"I meant to congratulate you. I did, really. I'm sorry
you took it the wrong way because I didn't. It's just that
I've had a lot on my mind lately."

My heart gave an extra beat. "You mean about what
you told me last night? How Michael's sort of like
Gram's kittens?"

It was so unusual for Kim to have anything on her
mind that when she said she did it really got my attention. Not that my sister's an airhead or anything. It's that
she's a person who doesn't usually worry about stuff. Not
like me.

Sometimes, I lie awake at night and worry till I'm a
nervous wreck. About my chest, for instance. It still looks
like Joey's. Sometimes I think I'll never get boobs, that I'll
have to ask Mom to take me to a doctor to find out if
there's something wrong with my genes.

Kim shrugged. Then, in a typical Kimberlee Ann
Connelly way, she smoothed her bedspread till it looked
perfect before turning to me with a big smile. Suddenly,
she was Miss Congeniality again. She reached out to give
me a hug.

"Sarah Sarah*Sarah!*" she exclaimed. "You're always
such a little old lady about everything! Don't worry so
much. Things will be fine."

Things will be fine? What did that mean? They'd been fine when she and Michael first came home from St. Alban's. Exactly what "things" was she talking about now?

But Kim ran downstairs before I could ask, and a little while later I heard the doors of Michael's small green car slam shut and the two of them were gone for the day. Maybe they were going to drive around the countryside, stop at the Old Mill for something to eat. Maybe they'd sit in a shadowy corner by themselves and there'd be a candle on the table. I was glad. It would be a perfect place for Kim to get her ring—and after that she wouldn't worry anymore about whatever she said was on her mind. She'd know how much Michael loved her. That's what mattered most.

When they weren't back by suppertime, I asked Mom what the scoop was. "It's such a lovely day they said something about maybe driving over to visit Uncle Ralph and Maddy," she said. They weren't back by bedtime either, which I thought was definitely a good sign.

For once I slept late the next morning. When I woke, Kim was gone; her bed was made, and I could hear Dad and Joey outside. As I grabbed some clean shorts out of the box I'd put in Kim's closet, I saw something shiny on her bedside table. The promise ring! Its gold and silver hands were as pretty as I remembered. So Michael had given it to her. I put it on my own finger, where it was so loose it slipped around. I was so happy I hugged myself. It was plain the reason Kim didn't wear it to the Kwik Pik this morning was because it needed to be sized.

After we'd finished all our chores in the afternoon, Joey and Michael took the *Guinevere* out to fish for bass, which meant I didn't have a chance to ask Michael privately about what Kim said when he gave her the ring. After Dad and I worked Dandy Randy and Web for a while—because you can't slack off on training just because a dog wins in a show—I decided to ride my bike into town to see Katie.

Riding our bikes into Meadowville, coasting like racers down the long hill into town, was something Joey and I used to do almost every day in the summer. It felt kind of funny to be doing it all by myself. Now that Joey had Michael, though, he hardly cared if he ever saw Skippy Simpson so there was no reason for him to go into Meadowville anymore.

I laid my bike down under the maple tree in Katie's front yard, where the grass was all worn off because there are six kids in her family and somebody's been laying a bike down there for a kazillion years. I went around to the back door. I expected Katie's mom to answer.

But it was Emily who pushed the screen open with her knee. She was wearing denim cutoffs, a yellow shrink top, and was as tan and skinny as she used to be. I almost fell over when I saw what she was holding.

A baby!

"Uh, hi, Em," I said. The sight of the lump she held as if it were a loaf of fresh-baked bread made me nervous. What do you say to your best friend's sister, a person everybody whispered about in school, who's just had a baby even though she isn't married?

"I guess you, um, had it, huh?" I said weakly.

"She's not an it, Sarah," Emily said, and smiled down at whatever was in the blanket with a bemused expression, as if she were still getting used to what it was herself.

"Can I see?" I asked.

"Sure. C'mon in. Katie'll be back in a minute. She

just ran down to the Kwik Pik to get me some dispos-
ables." Emily was as pretty in her way as Kim was—tall
and lean, where my sister was small and dainty. Once
upon a time, the biggest concern in Em's life was her ca-
reer as Meadowville's best girl basketball player.

I followed Em into the living room and we sat on the
couch. She folded back the fuzzy pink blanket. Lying
there was a wrinkled little thing with tufts of dark hair
and squinched-up eyes, who looked sort of like a sleepy
monkey.

"Isn't she a dollface?" Emily murmured.

"No kidding," I agreed. "What's her name?" To be
honest, I wouldn't exactly have called her a dollface,
though I supposed babies improved with time.

"Marilee, with two *e*'s."

Wouldn't you know it. The kid got a name with flair,
and two *e*'s thrown in for luck.

"So are you coming back to school to graduate next
year?" I asked, which wasn't any of my business. I noticed Em didn't look like a person who was trying to get
back across an invisible line anymore. She looked like she
knew exactly who she was, where she was, and what she
intended to do next.

"Of course," she said briskly. "It's not as if my life's
ruined just because I've got a baby to take care of now. I'll
need all the education I can get, though, so as soon as I get
my diploma I'll start right in at the vo-tech. The quicker
I get a job, the better. I'll stay here with Mom and Dad till
I do, then after a while maybe I'll move somewhere. To
Milwaukee, maybe."

"I thought you wanted to apply for a scholarship at
Old Dominion," I reminded her, which was in Virginia
and famous for its girls' basketball team.

"I did," she admitted. I didn't hear any huge regret in

her voice. "But that was then. I've got Marilee to think about now. At vo-tech I'll major in computer science, because I—"

She would've told me more boring details about her life plans, but Katie barged in right then, her arms loaded with Huggies. She didn't look especially overjoyed to see me.

"Geez, Sarah! I thought you'd died out there at Brookfield and your folks had buried you under one of the dog runs," she grumbled.

"Listen, I'm sorry I haven't called you or had you out for a sleepover," I said. "But Kim dragged this guy home for the whole summer and there's no place left in the house to sleep anyone else." The explanation was enough to soften Katie's expression and she plunked down beside us on the sofa.

"Why's your sister need to drag guys home?" Katie asked, looking down at Em's baby with approval. I calculated her relationship to the sleepy little monkey: Katie was an aunt now. It was hard to imagine a person being an aunt when she hadn't even started seventh grade yet.

"Because when I was at the Kwik Pik just now the place was full of Kimmy's old Romeos," Katie went on. "She wasn't exactly fighting them off with a stick either."

I was so shocked the only thing I could think of was to lean over Marilee and join Katie and Em in admiring her. "Oh, such an itsy-bitsy dollface," I crooned as if I really believed it. Then I jumped off the sofa as if I'd just noticed a scorpion on it.

"Listen, you guys, I gotta go. Mom wanted me to pick up some stuff for supper"—it was another one of those fibs that I seemed to tell so easily—"so I better get back home or she'll shoot me."

"We've still got beds here," Katie said as she followed me out the back door. "Why don't you come for a sleepover real soon? Like how about this weekend? Camilla's coming over. She's got a new two-piece—green with black stripes—and we're going swimming at the rec center."

Then she added slyly, "Jason's back from vacation. Maybe he'll be there too."

"I'll call you," I promised, and yanked my bike upright. I figured I might be too busy for sleepovers and certainly too busy to think about Jason Conrad. I waved good-bye and pedaled straight to the Kwik Pik.

I went in and skulked noiselessly down the aisle with pretzels, chips, and beef jerky snacks, where I could see the checkout counter without being seen myself.

The old Romeos must've cleared out because the place was empty except for Dylan Irving, who was leaning across the counter. Kim used to go out with him when she was a senior in high school. I hadn't seen Dylan in a long time and was surprised that he still looked the same. Not movie star handsome, but cute. Kim leaned toward him. She smiled into his eyes as if they were talking about something really important.

When I stepped around the corner, knocking some beef jerky into the aisle, Kim straightened up and looked at me as if she'd never seen me before and I'd come to rob the place.

"Sarah! I didn't see you come in!" Surprise. She'd been so busy eyeballing Dylan Irving I could've snitched all the beef jerky I wanted and made a clean getaway. Her cheeks turned the color of ripe tomatoes, and she hastily began to straighten a rack of out-of-state maps beside the cash register.

"Obviously," I said.

"Did Mom send you in to get something?" she asked, ignoring Dylan Irving as she spritzed glass cleaner all over the countertop and polished it as if it were filthy.

"No. I came by because I was on my way home from Katie's and I just stopped, that's all." I frowned at Dylan Irving, gave Kim another scowl, went out, and got back on my bike.

The road home seemed a lot longer than it'd been coming into town. Plus, I had to pedal up the long hill, which was a lot more work than flying down it.

The sun was hot. I started to sweat. My legs ached. Finally, I got off and pushed the bike the rest of the way. When I reached the top, I climbed back on and pedaled slowly toward Brookfield.

I couldn't figure out how to think about what I was trying to think about. Finally, I realized it came down not to what *I* thought, but what Michael would think. Except who was going to tell him Kimmy was flirting with Dylan Irving?

Not me.

Besides, what was there to tell? Kim had gone to school in Meadowville from kindergarten through twelfth grade. She'd always been one of the most popular people in her class. Was secretary of the Booster Club; played the lead in *My Fair Lady*; was editor of the school paper. She had a ton of friends. Lots of them were boys. Anyway, what's so terrible about talking to an old boyfriend that a person's known since forever?

Nothing's wrong with it, Sarah S. Stupido, I told myself. Deep down, though, that's not how I felt.

Mom told me once that I had phases. Girls my age did, she said. They had something to do with hormones. Maybe Kim had phases too. Mom said people got over them. Kim would. She'd better. She'd better get that ring sized too, and start wearing it like she was supposed to. If she needed money to pay for the sizing, I'd loan her some out of my allowance. I wouldn't even charge her interest.

chapter twelve

When the phone rang I was right there in the front hall next to the phone stand, so I picked it up.

I recognized Dylan Irving's voice right away. It didn't seem all that long ago that he'd called Kim practically every night. Back then, I used to answer and just hand the phone to her, holding my nose as if I smelled something horrible. Just what you'd expect a pesky little sister on TV to do.

"Hi, Sarah," Dylan said before I could grab my nose. "Does Kim happen to be around?" I would've said no, but she was standing in the kitchen, watching me like a hawk, a question in her eyes.

Is it Dylan? she mouthed silently, so no one else could hear.

Yes, I mouthed back, and held out the phone with one hand as I reached for my nose with the other.

"Grow up, Sarah!" she hissed, and turned her back on me. She tucked the phone close under her chin and began to murmur into it like she did when she was in high school. But she wasn't in high school anymore. She was supposed to be practically grown up. Someone had even given her a promise ring and asked her to get married.

"*You* grow up!" I spit in her ear before I slammed the front door behind me.

I was so mad I wanted to clobber her. Yet it was hard to explain my feelings, even to myself. Two and a half months ago, when Michael Miller first showed up at Brookfield, I was so hateful because he'd taken over my room that I wasn't fit to live with.

Now, it was different. The question was, *why?* Michael was still in my room. I was still on a cot in a dark corner of Kim's. I still hadn't had a single sleepover. Jason Conrad still hadn't come to watch videos. Except that none of those things mattered, because—

Dad called to me from the shed, interrupting my search for some whys and wherefores. "Sarah, I think I've got a surprise for you," he said, beckoning to me. To protect his back till it healed, he used a back brace that cinched with Velcro fasteners around his middle and had suspenders over the shoulders, the kind shelf stockers in grocery stores wear.

I wished there was someone I could tell about what Kim was doing. Would Dad understand? Except what would I tell him? She hadn't actually done anything.

"You won't believe it, Sarah, but I think Bingo might be coming around," Dad said.

"How come?" I asked. The news was so great I forgot about Kim and Dylan for a minute. "What'd you do to him?"

"It's not anything I did," Dad said. "It's just Bingo-boy himself. I think he's coming out of his shell." He grinned and we went down to run number 17. He opened Bingo's gate and clipped a lead onto his collar.

"An old-time trainer told me once that dogs can be

sort of like teenagers," he explained. "They go through certain phases." Even dogs had phases? "They get moody and uncertain and can't explain their feelings any more than a teenager can. Then, one day they turn back into their old confident selves again." His words made me feel a little better about Kim.

I followed Dad down to the arena, where he started gaiting Bingo. It was like watching a brand-new dog. Bingo moved as easily as water over smooth stones, fluid and effortless. The sunlight slanting through the dusty windows made his coat gleam like ebony. When Dad stacked him, Bingo held his pose as if he'd been doing it for years.

Dad looked at me with twinkly eyes. "Remember what I said when Bingo first came to Brookfield?" he asked.

How could I forget? "'Bingo! I think we've got a winner here,'" I said.

"And I'll say it again," Dad told me. "I think this guy may be just as much Westminster material as Web is." He winked at me. "Maybe we'll go there together, Sarah. You with Web, me with Bingo."

"Or maybe the other way around," I teased, because Bingo was still my favorite. With Dad so happy, it seemed like an okay time to talk not only about animals that had phases but people who did.

"Did you and Mom ever have second thoughts about getting married?" I asked. He laughed out loud and whacked his knee.

"Sure! I think it's natural. They call it wedding bell blues. After all, a person's starting a whole different life. I think your mother had more second thoughts than I did, though. I knew she was the girl for me the minute I laid eyes on her." He gave me a curious look. "What makes you ask, Sarah?"

"Nothing," I fibbed. But I decided to ask Mom too, which I did in the kitchen ten minutes later, as she finished making a batch of snickerdoodles.

"After you said you'd marry Dad, did you ever get a case of wedding bell blues?" She passed the empty mixing bowl to me so I could lick it.

"Of course," she said, and laughed just like Dad did. "I think everyone does. Although I think in our case it was your dad who had more second thoughts than I did."

Okay, it must be natural, even if people couldn't remember later who had the most second thoughts. Maybe I could quit worrying about Kim and Michael. Anyway, hadn't Kim herself told me not to be an old granny about stuff?

When Kim and Michael set off for their walk around the lake after supper, I watched them go. They were holding hands. A good sign. Kim kept her head bent, and Michael leaned down and seemed to be talking to her about something really important. Maybe about where they'd live after they got married. I'd already scoped out Kim's bedside table. The ring was gone, another good sign. She must've wrapped yarn around the band to make it fit better till she got it sized.

I dropped off to sleep before they got back. When I woke, I glanced at the clock I kept on the floor beside my cot. It was past midnight. Then I heard funny noises coming from Kim's bed. It sounded to me as if she might be sick to her stomach. If she was going to upchuck I decided I better go get Mom. It took me another second to realize my sister was crying.

"What's wrong?" I whispered. "Is it about— Michael?" I asked, dread making my heart rattle and my hands get clammy.

"P-p-partly," she sniffled.

Only partly. Then I remembered Dylan's call. I thought about the serious look on her face when she tucked the phone under her chin, how her nose got red as if she were going to cry. That's when Dylan must've told her that since she was practically engaged to Michael it'd be best if they didn't talk to each other anymore.

Pity began to nibble at my heart. I knew it was hard to let go of people you've always liked, because before Katie was my best friend Allie Jones was. She moved away to Texas when we were in second grade. It's like saying good-bye to part of your life when you have to let go of someone. So in spite of how mad I'd been at Kim lately, I felt a little sympathy for her.

I sat up on the edge of my cot. Kim was curled up in a ball in the middle of her bed, even though it was the middle of August and way too warm to curl up in a ball.

"Is it about Dylan, then?" I asked. He might've also admitted that he had a girl in Chicago or Milwaukee or wherever and they were going steady. Maybe he'd even given her a promise ring, just like Michael gave Kim.

The lump in the bed didn't answer. "S-s-sort of," she said at last. I climbed off my cot and tiptoed closer, but I didn't sit down.

"It'll be okay, Kim," I whispered, and reached out to pat her on the hip. It's easy to get mad at a sister but mostly the girls I know love their sisters. Like Katie loved Em, even though kids at school sometimes said mean things about her. Most of the time I loved Kim too.

"You want to talk about it?" I kneeled beside her bed as if I intended to pray over her.

Kim rolled over; in the greenish glow from the yard light outside I could see her cheeks were shiny and wet. There was a mountain of used-up tissues next to her pillow.

"It's just so hard, Sare-Bear," she whispered. She must feel really, truly terrible, because she hadn't called me Sare-Bear since I was a little kid.

"What's hard?"

"Falling in love. Falling out of love."

After seeing Dylan again at the Round House with the old gang, Kim must've remembered how much she'd liked him once. Maybe for a while she fell a little bit in love with him all over again. It must've been Dylan who came to his senses first, so now her heart was feeling a little bit broken.

Never in her entire life had my sister ever been dumped by a guy. Now it had finally happened. On the phone this afternoon Dylan probably told her about the other girlfriend. No wonder she was crying. Something like that was probably really painful to a person who wasn't used to it. My sister didn't have much experience being a dumpee; she'd always been the dumper.

"Want me to crawl in with you?" I asked. She didn't answer but wiggled over to make room for me. "We used to sleep together on the screen porch up at Gram's cottage, remember?" I said as I crept under the sheet beside her. "But you always hogged all the blankets."

Kim giggled and made watery, snuffly sounds. "And you got the sheets gritty because you'd never wash the sand off your feet." She reached for a tissue and blew her nose hard, making loud honking sounds.

"You know what, Sare?" she asked, then was silent. I waited for her to go on. "I just wish . . . I just wish . . ." Her words trailed off again.

"You wish what?" I coaxed.

"I wish . . . I wish I loved Michael the way I did at the beginning of summer," she said.

I sat straight up beside her. "You don't . . . love

Michael . . . anymore?" I felt cool all over. My heart pounded in a funny, scared way.

"What I feel is—well, Sare, I feel *sorry* for Michael. So sorry. Because of what happened to Matthew. Because of how Michael blames himself for what was only an accident. He can't forgive himself, and it's a load that's almost too heavy for him to carry." She paused. "The truth is, it's too heavy for me too. Because you know something, Sare? Being sorry for a person isn't the same as loving them."

"But you *have* to love him, Kim!" I said through gritted teeth. "You guys said you were going to get married." I started to talk so fast I didn't stop to bother with punctuation.

"You told Mom and Dad you were so they told Gram and Gramp and three days ago I heard Mom tell someone in her quilt club that you guys were getting married after graduation and besides don't forget Michael gave you that promise ring and I'll loan you money to get it sized if it doesn't fit just right because Michael told me a promise ring is what a guy gives a girl before he buys her the real one that's got diamonds and anyway there's such a thing as wedding bell blues because I asked Mom and Dad and they said so and now everybody expects the two of you will go ahead and—"

"I can't marry Michael, Sarah," Kim said, putting the name Sare-Bear back in storage. She was still sniffling, but there was an end-of-the-romance sound in her voice.

"I wish I could, for his sake. I don't ever want to hurt him, Sarah. Not ever. Michael's already been through the mill. But it'd be wrong to let him go on thinking we're ever really going to be married. That'd be dishonest. I can't do it."

"Does Michael know about this yet?"

"I-I-I'm not sure," she murmured sadly.

"What's that mean?"

"It means we've talked about it. Sort of. About not going ahead with our plans right away. But I didn't say for sure that I didn't want to, not ever."

"When're you going to tell him?"

"Soon. I have to. It'll be best for everyone." She paused. "He'll probably decide to leave Brookfield. That means you can have your room back, Sarah."

I flopped down beside her, and when Kim reached for my hand I let her curl our fingers together like we did when we slept at Gram's cottage. I stared at the ceiling. At night the paint looked white instead of peach colored. My head and heart felt as hollow as empty buildings.

Kim didn't love Michael Miller anymore. The hugeness of the news weighed me down like a boulder in the pit of my stomach. She'd loved him when she brought him home in June, but she'd changed her mind and now she didn't. As I listened to her sniffle, I realized how bad she felt about what'd happened.

I couldn't explain that it was a big problem for me too. Because I didn't want my summer back anymore. Not my room either. What I wanted was for Michael to be part of our family, just like Kim said he was going to be.

Kim didn't love Michael anymore? Well, now I did.

Not like a boyfriend, but like a person I wanted to belong to the Connellys for keeps. Not because I felt sorry for him either, like Kim said she did. Maybe I loved him because he knew lots of stuff about King Arthur or because he knew how to joust or because he was so nice to Joey. Or just because he was Michael. Love is hard to explain to anyone, especially to yourself.

When I was sure Kim was asleep, I sneaked out of

bed. I looked down at her. She had her hands crossed over her chest; I looked close to see if she was wearing the promise ring. She wasn't. I looked on the table beside her bed. There it was, back on its blue velvet cushion.

I pulled on a pair of old jeans and a sweatshirt, tip-toed into the hall, and stood outside my old room. At the end of the hall, Joey's night-light shed a pale glow on the floor. Slowly I opened the door of my old room a crack. I couldn't decide if I hoped Michael was awake or asleep.

The bed was smooth. There was nobody in it. Michael wasn't leaning out my window either. I peered around the room. It was empty.

I closed the door and waited alone in the hall for a minute, then went silently down the stairs into the kitchen. The refrigerator hummed a comforting tune as I walked past it and out the back door.

From the porch I could see Michael on the dock. In the light of the half-moon his silver hair looked more like a medieval helmet than ever. If I went down there to join him, what would I say?

Gee, Michael, Kim just told me the latest. Sorry about that. Guess she just doesn't love you anymore.

Or, *There are lots of fish in the ocean, Michael. Go catch another one. Forget about my sister.*

Or, *I don't need my room back. Stay the rest of the sum-mer. You can still help us with Bingo and Chessie and Web and all the other mutts.*

I headed for the dock. It'd be okay with me if we just sat side by side and didn't say a word. Bare feet on wet grass at night make even less noise than they do in day-time, so it was only the creaking of the dock when I stepped on it that made Michael turn around. He smiled that smile that wasn't really a smile at all, just a quirky upturn of the corners of his mouth.

"You must be Sarah," he said. The same words he'd said that very first day. In the same mild, thoughtful voice that made me want to give him a hug.

"It was hot. I couldn't sleep," I muttered.

"But it's great out here," he said, lifting his arms over his head. "Feel that air coming down from the north. Almost cold, but not quite. Means autumn can't be far away."

Beside us, the *Guinevere* gently butted against the rubber tire Dad had tied to the dock to keep her paint from getting rubbed off. In front of us, the lake was the color of pewter and was neither smooth nor rough.

"Did Kim tell you?" Michael asked quietly after I sat down beside him.

"Tell me what?" I hedged.

"Well, Sarah, I don't think your sister feels the same way about me as she did at the beginning of summer." He seemed calm and not especially brokenhearted. "I still love *her,* though. I'd still like to get married. I think if we could just—"

"It's all that stupid Dylan Irving's fault," I blurted.

Michael leaned against me in a gentle protest. "It's not Dylan's fault, Sarah. He didn't do anything." He was silent for a while, and when he started to talk again it was in a dreamy sort of voice.

"The thing is, I can't imagine my life without Kim in it. She's just—so—so alive. So warm. That's what I noticed first about her. You're like that too, Sarah. Your folks. Joey. All you guys helped me to believe that—" He paused and sighed.

I guess I took being alive for granted. It never occurred to me the Connellys were all that special just because they breathed. Then I said something that shocked me a lot more than it shocked Michael Miller.

"Michael, wait for me."

The words sounded as if they came out of the mouth of someone I didn't know. But the minute I said them I knew it could be the perfect way to keep him in the family.

"I'll grow up as fast as I can," I rushed on. "It won't take too long. I'll be in seventh grade next year. Kim's not the only Connelly girl you could marry. If you want, I'll even start reading King Arthur stories again. After a while maybe you'd feel the same way about me as you do about Kim. All you have to do is wait, Michael."

Michael laughed. Not one of those laughs that makes you feel as if someone wants to embarrass you. It was a sweet, tender laugh, like a kindly old uncle might give you. Michael looped his arm around my shoulder and gave me a squeeze.

"Nobody's ever asked me to wait for them before. And you know something, Sarah? I'll never forget you're the one who did."

chapter thirteen

Two days later, when we were right in the middle of eating tuna sandwiches for lunch, Gram called about Gramp's accident. After that, none of us had time to think about anything else. Not even about what Kim had told Michael the day before.

Gramp had taken a ladder to climb up on the roof of the cottage so he could check the chimney for birds' nests. There weren't any, but when he started back down he fell all the way into the petunia bed after only the first two rungs.

It wasn't because there was anything wrong with the rungs on the ladder, though. The doctor told Gramp he'd had a TIA. Gram explained the initials meant "transient ischemic attack," which is like a tiny stroke. It wasn't bad enough to ruin Gramp's speech or make him weak on one side, so he'd have to use a cane. Just enough to warn him that now he'd need certain kinds of medicine to keep him from having any more TIAs.

"We'll be back sometime this evening," Mom said as she and Dad and Joey got ready to climb into the van and take off after we finished our tuna sandwiches. "We'll need to make sure Gram has plenty of home-nursing care till Gramp gets back on his feet. We'll eat supper with them at the hospital, so you two kids help yourselves to whatever's left in the fridge. We'll be back in time to help Michael get ready for the plane in the morning."

"Sarah, make sure you stick around to answer the phone in case we get some calls about boarders," Dad reminded me.

"How come I can't stay here with Michael and Sarah?" Joey asked wistfully, tugging on his lower lip. I knew he was thinking the same thing I was: Michael would be gone in such a short time. Maybe neither one of us would ever see him again.

It was Dad who made it easier for Joey. "We'll be home in plenty of time for you to see Michael before he leaves," he soothed. "But the last time we went to Gram and Gramp's you were off on that camping trip with Skippy and his folks. I think it'd be a real boost for Gramp's spirits if he could see you today, buddy."

Before they drove out of the yard Dad gave Michael a special hug, even though it wasn't their final parting yet. "About Kim," I heard him say softly as he drew Michael aside and placed a brown hand between Michael's shoulder blades. "A broken romance isn't the end of the world, son. Remember, we all like you just for yourself. You'll be welcome at Brookfield any time you want to come back."

My mother didn't just pat Michael. Her eyes got all shiny with tears and she kissed him on both cheeks, which made him turn pink under his tan. Then Joey grabbed him around the waist like he did the day Michael jousted with the liver-colored stray.

"Don't forget you still owe me a game of chess," he mumbled against Michael's belt buckle.

To make the parting easier for everyone—in my opinion she was thinking of herself most of all—Kim decided to stay in town for a few days with her old crony, Melinda.

Melinda! That rat. That weasel. That candidate for Skunk of the Year award. I hated how she bragged she'd gone to college to major in boys. Boys and having a good time were all she ever thought about.

If she'd never invited my sister to come to that party at the Round House, maybe Kim would still love Michael the way she had at the beginning of summer. I prayed when Melinda got back to school nobody'd ever ask her for a date again, that boys would treat her as if she smelled like the mouse we couldn't get out from behind the kitchen sink after it died.

"Well, partner, shall we get to work?" Michael asked after Mom and Dad and Joey turned the corner at the mailbox and disappeared down the county road. He didn't seem gloomy, like I was afraid he might be. "I'll do the kennels as usual, while you take care of whatever it is you need to take care of."

It was a relief to see he was handling things so well, which, considering how pale and beat down he'd looked for two days after Kim laid the bad news on him, was a big surprise. When he glanced at me, his bottle-blue eyes were as calm and clear as a baby's. His smile actually was more cheerful than the usual quirky upturning of his lips that I'd gotten used to. It was an almost-happy smile, which made it extra hard for me to remember that once I'd vowed to make his life miserable.

"After we get through, and all the dogs have been

exercised, let's have a picnic down on the dock," I suggested, since he was in such a good mood. At first, Michael didn't seem interested in the idea, then I thought he looked sort of pleased.

"Sort of a going-away celebration, just for you and me," I explained, to convince him. "Because you're the person who made it possible for Dad and me to work together this summer. You're the reason I got a red ribbon, Michael. And maybe it's why Bingo shaped up. Dad had more time to spend with him because you were here to help us out."

Michael smiled and ruffled my hair the way he sometimes ruffled Joey's. I wondered if he might give me a hug too, but he didn't. "You've got a big heart, Sarah. You think of everything," he said. Of course, I'd never told him about my Welcome to Siberia plot. Then I realized what I'd miss most when Michael was gone: how my name sounded when he said it.

Sarah. It was better than a hug, and I tried not to think I might never hear him say it again. Beginning with that very first day, when he stood in the entryway, he made it sound so special. Not plain at all. I knew for sure I'd never go to court to change it for anything. Not even to something with two *e*'s. Kimberlee and Marilee could have all the double vowels they wanted.

It took us most of the afternoon to get everything done. After each of the dogs had been walked for ten minutes apiece, it was past suppertime. I rummaged through the fridge and found some chicken wings and drummies, some potato salad, and pickles. I peeled two oranges, got some taco chips, and a couple candy bars. I stuck everything, including napkins, paper plates, and some pop, in a paper sack and we headed for the dock.

Before Dad left he'd warned me that the cell phone

was on the fritz, so I hauled the regular kitchen phone out to the back porch. I turned the bell to "loud" and set the phone on a tin pie plate turned upside down so it'd make more noise in case we got any calls about boarders.

"Want to take the *Guinevere* out so we can have our picnic on the water?" I asked Michael when we got to the end of the dock. Just before sunset, the wind often was perfect, about four or five miles an hour.

"My, my what a short memory you've got!" he teased. "Don't forget, you've gotta listen for the phone," he reminded me, jerking his thumb in the direction of the back porch. "Anyway, it's okay with me if we just sit here and watch the sun go down." We took off our shoes and dangled our feet in the water. As we watched, it began to turn the color of grape juice as the sun got lower.

We didn't talk for a while, even though there was a ton of stuff I wanted to say. There was one thing in particular. Finally, I got up enough nerve.

"Have you thought about what I said, Michael. About waiting for me?" I asked.

He chuckled softly. "Oh, Sarah, don't be in a rush to grow up just because of me."

"Well, then, can we at least be friends forever and ever?" I asked, taking a chicken wing out of the sack. "Even though now you and Kim are—well, you know."

"Of course we can be friends, Sarah. Forever, if you'd like to."

"Will you write to me after you get back to St. Albans?"

"Do you want me to?" Michael murmured, taking a pickle and nudging my ankle with his toe.

"It'd be neat to have you for a pen pal," I said. "I won't care if Joey teases me or even if he tries to read the letters before he gets 'em back from the mailbox. And if you find out some new stuff about King Arthur or Lancelot or Guinevere you can write me about it."

"And you could let me know how Bingo's coming along," he said, as if the idea of trading letters was beginning to appeal to him. "Be sure to tell me if Web gets any closer to Westminster and if Dan ever takes a hammer to that hardheaded Chessie. Most especially, be sure to tell me if you come across some more legends about Loon Woman."

I was glad he didn't say he wanted to hear anything about Kim.

I cleared my throat. "I heard Dad say you could come back anytime," I said. "Do you think you will? Like next summer, maybe? Dad might even let you start handling dogs yourself."

"We'll see, Sarah. We'll see." I was sorry his answer sounded like the no-answer kind grown-ups give kids.

After that, we didn't talk much, but that was the nice thing about Michael. You didn't feel as if you had to. He nudged my ankle every now and then and sometimes I leaned my shoulder into his. Once, he lifted his arm to cradle me under his armpit and even gave me a kiss on top of my head.

I was halfway through my third chicken wing when I heard the rattle of the phone against the pie plate on the porch.

"Wouldn't you know it," I groaned, and took off at a dead run. If somebody wanted to talk about boarding their dog I'd set up an appointment for tomorrow when Dad was home so they could bring their pooch out. For sure I didn't want anyone coming out now and ruining my party with Michael. "I'll find out who it is and be right back," I called over my shoulder.

But it wasn't anybody wanting to board a mutt or

anything else to do with dogs. It was dim Kim, which made me so mad my chicken wings almost flapped right out of my stomach.

"Is everything all right?" she asked.

"What do you mean, 'is everything all right?'" I snapped. "After what you did? Anyway, why wouldn't it be? If it's any business of yours, Michael and I are having a picnic. Mom said we could eat anything we wanted out of the fridge, so that's what we're doing."

I glanced over my shoulder toward the dock. Michael had stood up and was looking back at me. I covered the phone and yelled, "It's just Katie, Michael. I'll be back in a minute." If he knew it was Kim, he might want to talk to her, which would make him feel gloomy.

"How's Michael?" she asked.

"'How's Michael,'" I mimicked. "He's fine," I said through clenched teeth. "What I want to know is how come you're so concerned all of a sudden. *You* are the one who wouldn't wear the promise ring. *You* are the one who didn't want to talk about getting married anymore. As far as I know, Michael never ragged on you about Dylan Irving, did he? No. He never said he wanted to break up with you, did he? No. So now what's the big hairy deal, Kim?"

"It's just that I . . . well, Sare, I feel so guilty." For a second I hated her for using my old nickname. If we'd been talking face-to-face I might've poked her smack in the nose.

"I never wanted to hurt Michael. But it wasn't fair to let him go on believing we'd get married someday when I knew in my heart it could never happen."

"Trust me, Kim, Michael's okay with this," I assured her. "He hasn't mentioned anything about you or getting married or any of that stuff. For all you know, maybe he's already thinking about somebody else at St. Alban's. You're not the only girl on campus, y'know."

The fact it might be true made my heart feel a little pinched, so I added icily, "Remember, you're not the only one who knows how to love a person." I was referring to myself, of course, not to anyone at St. Alban's. "Maybe Michael doesn't miss you as much as you thought he would. Ever think of that?"

"Please don't be so mad at me, Sarah," Kim begged.

I hesitated before answering. "Well I am, if you want to know the truth. You're the one who decided to bring Michael home for the entire summer, right? You're the one who never asked me or Joey if we had any plans, right? Then everybody got used to him. Even me. Everyone liked him—Gram and Gramp too—" I paused to take a breath.

"Then *you* decided you'd made a mistake, that Michael couldn't get over what happened to Matthew. So the rest of us are s'posed to delete him like he's a file on somebody's disk drive that nobody needs anymore? Give me a break, Kim!"

"Don't be so mean," she murmured. I heard her begin to sniffle on the other end of the line. "You make it sound as if I'm a cold, terrible person with no heart."

"Well, maybe that's exactly what you are, Kim." I was tired of listening to her explain and complain.

"Michael's waiting for me," I said. "My potato salad's probably getting warm. In health science we learned how eating food on picnics after it gets above a certain temperature is the way people get food poisoning. I might die if I don't go back and eat it right now." I hung up.

Sheesh. Then I heard Bingo barking out in the kennel shed. I could always tell his deep, resonant voice from the other mutts'. Maybe he'd like to be included in our farewell picnic. I loped out to the shed, grabbed his collar and a lead off the Peg-Board behind the door, and started back to the dock.

I was surprised to see Michael wasn't where I'd left him. Then I realized the *Guinevere* wasn't tied up at the dock either. I shaded my eyes against the lowering sun and scanned the lake. Close to the Deep, I could see the *Guinevere*'s mainsail, a ghostly white triangle, in the falling light.

I cupped my hands around my mouth. "Why didn't you wait for me, Michael?" I called. "How come you went without—"

I didn't finish. Suddenly I felt cool all over. I remembered what Dad said when I asked him if people ever got over something like what happened to Matthew. *A reminder can bring the grief back . . .*

Bingo sat at my heel, straight up, attentive, his eyes trained on the *Guinevere* too, as if he'd forgotten he was afraid of water. I rested my fingertips on the top of his wide black head.

I saw Michael uncleat the mainsail. He stepped onto the bow of the *Guinevere*. I was the one who'd showed him how to dive off like that, though of course not in the middle of the lake where the water was so cold.

But he didn't dive right away. He paused, holding his arms straight out from his sides as if they were wings. His silver hair was as sleek to his head as a metal helmet. He'd gotten so tan over the summer that he looked like a strange island god carved out of teakwood.

"Wait, Michael!" I called, my hands around my mouth again. "It's too cold out there, Michael! That's why we always swim closer to shore . . ."

Bingo quivered against my knee. I hooked my hand under his collar. The *Guinevere*'s sail hung limp. The boat didn't move much, so I knew Michael had raised the centerboard.

I watched him lift himself in an arc off the hull of the *Guinevere*. For a second he was silhouetted against the crimson sky. Free. Held safely in place by invisible sky wires. Then he started his downward trajectory, slid into the black water with barely a splash, and vanished.

I waited for him to come up. He did, and held his hands over his head as if he were lifting something up to the sky for a special blessing.

He didn't come up a second time.

"Michael, wait for me!" I called again. I jumped off the dock onto the beach. I turned the old rowboat over, threw in the oars and life jackets that were stored underneath.

"In!" I hollered to Bingo, unclipping the lead from his collar. I shoved the boat into the water, waded out, and climbed in myself. I grabbed up the oars and started to row. Hard, hard, hard. Within moments my chest was on fire. My arms ached. Cold sweat trickled down my ribs.

Had Michael heard me? Were the last four words lingering in the air above his head my own?

Bingo and I were more than a hundred yards from the *Guinevere* when suddenly I was sure I saw fresh ripples on the water's surface.

Before I could say a word, Bingo hurled himself over the side of the rowboat as if he'd been shot out of a cannon. He swam with sure, steady strokes toward the *Guinevere,* his eyes fastened on the ever-expanding circles over the Deep that marked the place where Michael disappeared.

It took another minute or two for me to get to where Bingo paddled back and forth over the center of the

world. Soon the circles Michael made when he entered
the water were erased, expanding outward toward the
shore in rings that grew fainter and fainter, till they vanished altogether. The only stirring in the water was what
Bingo and I caused ourselves.

Far off, I heard a loon call.

The crimson sky deepened to burgundy.

I shivered.

I rested the oars in their locks and stared down. The
water was blacker than Bingo's coat. "Michael, Michael,"
I whispered in a voice that echoed like a stranger's in my
ears. "Why didn't you wait?"

But I knew I was talking to myself. Michael couldn't
hear me now.

I whistled Bingo to the side of the rowboat. I tried to
drag him aboard, but he was way too heavy for me to
haul over the side. The water was so cold it burned my
hands, and I felt Bingo shudder with exhaustion. I
snatched up a life jacket and fastened it around him as
best I could, then grabbed a rope from the bottom of the
boat and tied it to his collar.

I rowed toward shore, looking back every fifteen sec-
onds to make sure Bingo kept his head above water. I
couldn't lose him too. My thoughts tumbled over and
under each other. My breath came in jagged puffs. My
chest was sore. My arms ached worse than ever. The skin
across my forehead was stretched tight, making my eyes
feel weird. I didn't cry, though. Sometimes, when something terrible happens, a person can't.

I hauled the rowboat onto the beach and headed for
the house. Bingo hustled out of the water, shook himself,
then raced beside me to the back porch. I grabbed the
phone off the bottom step. Water leaked out of my
sneakers and ran in rivulets down the stone path toward

the kennel shed. I dialed 911 and explained to the dispatcher on the other end that there'd been an accident at Brookfield Boarding Kennel out on County Road Seven.

"My friend Michael fell off our boat in the middle of Echo Lake," I said. I gave her directions. "Send a rescue team—quick!"

But even as I begged her in a high voice that belonged to someone else to send help as fast as she could, I knew it was too late.

I hung up the phone. "Stay!" I commanded Bingo, and went into the kitchen. The refrigerator hummed its soothing tune. More water leaked out of my sneakers and made a puddle where I stood. I thought I might fly apart. Arms, legs, heart, head. All exploding away from me like parts of a broken machine.

I pressed my hands against my chest to hold myself together. My mother's words were the only ones that came to me. I repeated them silently, over and over, like a prayer. *Now, Sarah; now, Sarah.*

I went upstairs. The door of my old room was closed. I opened it and turned on the light. Michael's suitcase was packed and lay on the end of the bed. That's when I found out people do peculiar things at bad times in their lives. Because right then I looked up to see if the wild mustang's head was still on my ceiling. As if somehow Michael might have taken it away with him.

I walked to the open window, where Michael had leaned out to look across the lake or study the stars. Far down the county road I heard a siren. Faint at first, then growing louder, louder. The dogs in the kennel shed began to howl like wolves on a winter night. A moment later, Bingo called to me in a stricken voice from the back porch.

I turned and went downstairs. I knelt beside Bingo and hugged him hard. "It'll be all right, Bingo, Chingo, Dingo," I said, laying my face against his wet black neck. Then we walked together down to the county road to explain to the rescue team about the accident.

Except I lied to Bingo. I knew things would never be all right again. And I knew what happened hadn't been an accident.

chapter fourteen

"It's all *her* fault!" I yelled.

It made me crazy to see my sister sitting there on the couch next to Mom, hugging herself as if she were so cold she'd never get warm again. *She* wasn't the one who'd gone down, down, down into the icy Deep at the center of the world. It was Michael who had.

"She knew how bad Michael felt about what happened to his brother!" I screeched, pointing at Kim like an avenging angel descended from heaven above.

"She told me so herself! She said Michael talked about it lots of times and even cried when they walked around the lake!" I could feel heat rise inside me as if I were a pressure cooker.

"But what'd dim Kim go and do? She went and told Michael she wouldn't marry him. She should've known after what happened to Matthew he wouldn't be able to stand it. Losing someone he loved a second time would be too much. But she went and said it anyway!"

"Now, Sarah; now, Sarah," my mother said, putting her arm around Kim to protect her, as if my words were darts with steel tips. "You mustn't say such dreadful things." There was a beseeching note in her voice. I paid no attention.

"I will too say them! What happened is all because of Kim! She didn't like cleaning kennels either!" I shouted, as if that had anything to do with anything. "If she just hadn't gone and told Michael—"

Kim sat there as white as a sheet while I ranted. Her laughing eyes were dull and sad. Even her hair had lost its brightness and its lively curl.

"Michael's grief just got so heavy," she whispered in a thready voice. "It's true when we walked around the lake all he ever talked about was Matthew. He talked about him when he showed me the promise ring too. He said if I took it—if I'd promise to marry him—it'd help make up for how he felt about what'd happened to his brother." She twisted her hands in her lap. When she looked up at me her eyes were two blank windows in her white face.

"Lots of times he said he wished it'd been him who died. He said it wasn't fair Matthew had to be the one. Once, he even said he didn't want to go on living if Matthew couldn't live too."

I refused to believe Kim was trying to make sense out of what happened the same as I was.

"See, when I first met Michael I really thought I could make everything different for him. That I could make him be as happy as I was. It seemed so simple. But there was no way, and finally, finally . . ." Her voice trailed off into silence.

"If Kim hadn't called last night to ask how Michael was, I would've sat right there beside him on the dock and he'd never have climbed into the *Guinevere* by himself," I rattled on as if I hadn't heard a word she said. "Nothing bad would've happened. Michael would be alive this very minute instead of deader than—"

"Sarah!"

I hadn't seen Dad come in from outside. His voice reverberated from all four corners of the living room like a thunderclap. I was glad Joey was in town at Skippy Simpson's till arrangements could be made about Michael because the sound would've scared him out of a year's growth.

"Mother, you stay here with Kim. Sarah and I are going outside for a bit." When he called Mom *mother* like that, a person knew he was as serious as he ever got.

I followed him out the back door. He strode into the kennel shed without a word, his shoulders hunched up around his ears, then down the aisle toward the showring. The dogs sensed something different about both of us and didn't make a sound as we passed their pens. The early morning light filtered through the windows in the east wall and bathed the arena in a pale yellow glow.

"Sit down, Sarah," he commanded.

I sat on a bench along the wall.

"What happened to Michael is nobody's fault. It's certainly not Kim's. Not Michael's either. I won't have you laying blame on anyone in this matter," he declared, striding back and forth in front of me.

"It was an unfortunate accident that killed Matthew Miller, and what happened to Michael is terrible too. But none of it—*none of it, mind you*—was any of Kim's doing." He stopped in midstride and glared at me, his fists on his hips. "I won't have you punishing her, Sarah, or behaving like some celestial judge and jury."

Celestial judge and jury. I'd never heard my dad use words like that or talk to anybody in such a hard, sharp voice. I put my thumbs together and noticed my fingernails were still dirty from getting the rowboat turned over last night.

"Kim was the one who dragged him here in the first place," I insisted. "She's the one who made Michael think she would—"

"*Sarah!*" Dad boomed again. "Remember what I told you about that Chessie? That a Chesapeake could be handled tough or handled tender? Well, which way's it going to be with you?"

"I'm sorry," I muttered. Not because of Kim, though. I was sorry because I knew how disappointed he was in me.

He paced back and forth in front of me awhile longer, then finally sat on the bench next to me. Close, hip to hip, his shoulder touching mine. He took one of my hands in his.

"Each of us came to love Michael in our own way," he said, "and it always hurts to lose someone you care for, Sarah. Just try to remember the good times." His voice went suddenly soft. There was no more thunder and lightning in it, just a wistful tone that made me wish I could cry a little.

"What if there aren't good times?" I groaned. Because all I could think of was how Michael hadn't waited for me to get off the phone, to come back to the dock with Bingo. If he had—*if only he'd waited*—nothing this terrible would've happened. If he'd wanted to go out in the *Guinevere* one last time, I'd have gone with him. His grief wouldn't have had a chance to get the best of him.

"Michael told you so many things about King Arthur, remember? And you told him that old story about Loon Woman. He was such a big help in Milwaukee—in fact, we'd never have gotten there without him, Sarah. And don't forget, you're the one who helped him pick out that promise ring for Kim. Those were good times, Sarah, times when Michael was almost happy. They belong to you now that he's gone."

"That's not enough," I said in a voice as thready as Kim's. "I don't want to remember stuff like that. Stuff that's already happened. What I want is—" I licked my lips. "What I want is for Michael to come back. For the summer to go on just like it was."

"We all do, Sarah." Dad sighed and tilted his head against the wall behind us. "But there's no way in the world we can ever have Michael back. What's done is done."

Those were the worst words I'd ever heard. Worse than "dead." Worse than "suicide." *What's done is done.*

That's when I understood what it'd been like for Michael. He'd wanted to have Matthew back the same way I wanted him back. Except it was like Dad said: What had been done was done. Never in a million years could it be undone. Only that was something Michael couldn't accept whenever he remembered what'd happened to his brother.

"Now I want you to go back in the house and talk to Kim like a sister ought to," Dad said, and added extra pressure to his grip on my hand. "Kim feels as badly about this as anyone. She can't be blamed for doing what she believed was right, Sarah."

Mom and Kim were still on the couch when I went into the living room. I sat on the arm of Dad's old brown recliner. "I'm sorry, Kim," I said. "I shouldn't have said all that stuff. I know it's not your fault. I guess it's not anybody's."

She started to cry. I couldn't.

"Th-th-thank you, Sare-Bear," she said with a worn-out sniffle. I wanted to tell her—Mom too—that I'd never be Sare-Bear again. The summer had turned out to be about something a lot bigger than giving up a bedroom. It'd made me older than I'd ever been before. The same thing had happened to me as happened to Kim and Emily—something humongous and unexpected—and now I might never be able to find the person I used to be.

chapter fifteen

We Connellys hadn't been away from Brookfield together for a long time. Not since we went to Disneyland when Joey was only five and had to come home early because he got tonsillitis and had a temperature of a hundred and four.

But two days after what happened to Michael, Dad hired a man from town to come out and stay at Brookfield. He showed him how to feed and water the dogs and told him to be sure no mischief-making strays came skulking around hoping to make babies with our boarders.

Then the five of us got in the van and headed for the airport in Milwaukee to catch a morning flight to Indiana for the funeral.

After we got on the plane none of us cried, even though we knew we were going to say our final good-bye to Michael.

We'd already shed plenty of tears. Mostly when each of us was alone. At night in our beds, or else when we were doing our chores. Me, as I worked with Bingo and Web and Dandy Randy in the showring. Joey, when he cleaned kennels (he'd learned Michael's job so well he just shouldered it all by himself without even being asked). Kim, as she drove to the Kwik Pik to work (of course, she didn't use Michael's little green car anymore; she took Dad's pickup). Once, I saw Mom crying to herself as she made macaroni and cheese for supper. Though I didn't see Dad actually cry, he often had a faraway look in his eyes.

I didn't move back across the hall right away because Kim said she wanted me to stay right there on my lumpy cot in that gloomy corner of her room.

I said I would. I told her I didn't mind. I didn't either. Imagine. After the huge stink I raised about giving up my room for the summer; now, I didn't much care whether I ever moved back into it.

On the plane Kim and I sat together, while Mom and Dad and Joey sat across the aisle. She had the window seat and from the minute we took off she looked down at the marshmallow clouds, never saying a word. For a long time I didn't say anything either. It seemed like no matter how you put the words together, even if you used ones like "sad" or "tragic" or "terrible," none of them did justice to what had happened on Echo Lake.

Just the same, there *was* something I needed to say.

"Kim?" I said. I leaned toward her, pretending I wanted to see the clouds too. You'd think I'd still be mad at her, but after Dad and I had our talk my hatefulness began to leak out of me, a teaspoon at a time. Kim didn't answer right away.

"What?" she finally sighed into my ear in a weary voice.

"I know Michael didn't really mean to do it, Kim."

"What makes you so sure?" My sister's voice had always been as bright as her hair; now there were only

shades of gray and brown in it. "It's what Michael told me
himself he might do. More than once he said he didn't
want to go on living if Matthew couldn't too."

Mom and Dad still called what happened to Michael
an accident when they spoke of it to us kids, mostly for
Joey's sake, I think. When Kim and I were alone we
never did. That was okay for the rest of the family or for
the police who did the investigation or for people in
Meadowville—but she and I knew better.

"It's just this feeling I have, Kim. That if Michael had
taken ten more minutes to think about what he was
doing, he never would've—"

"But I keep blaming myself," Kim interrupted, her
voice darker brown than ever. "What if you were right,
Sarah? I mean, maybe I should've gone ahead with our
plans to get married. Maybe I was just being selfish. . . ."
Her words trailed off and she stared out the window
again.

At first, that's what I believed too. That if only Kim
hadn't said anything it would've been all right, that she'd
wrecked everything by telling Michael she'd changed her
mind. I reached for Kim's hand. She let me take it, and we
linked our pinkies the way we did when we were little.

"Don't blame yourself, Kim. Maybe it's like you said.
Being sorry for a person's not the same as love."

"Love," she whispered. "Such an easy word to spell.
Maybe that's why people think it'll be easy to do too."

She sounded a little bit like Katie's sister did before
Marilee was born. Old, as if she already knew things a
person her age shouldn't know so soon.

"In the beginning I was sure I could love Michael back
to himself," Kim said, unlinking her pinkie and taking my
whole hand in hers. She squeezed it hard, as if she needed
something more substantial than a pinkie to hang on to.

"I believed I could make him forget what happened to Matthew. That when he was around us Connellys—I mean, we're so average—he'd somehow turn into a happy person like the rest of us. He'd be able to see that what happened to his brother wasn't his fault."

But sometimes there's no way to comfort a person, even though you try to. Like when Camilla first found out her parents were getting divorced she cried all the time. In gym class, in the girls' bathroom, on the bus home from school. Katie and I did everything we could think of to make her feel better. Except it's as if people like that can't really hear you. They can see your lips move, but the words are in some foreign language they don't understand. Then, after a while, they get things figured out inside their own heads. They finally quit crying and life goes on like it always did.

Till that very minute, though, leaning against Kim and looking out at the clouds, I hadn't realized Michael couldn't see past his pain. He thought it was going to last forever, that first he lost Matthew and then he lost Kim. To him, it must have seemed like the end of the world.

"Loving himself back to life wasn't anything Michael needed to do for me," Kim said with a sigh. "He had to do it for himself, Sarah. There was no way I could fix things from the outside."

The sun glinted off the plane's wings, but all I could see in my mind's eye was Michael on the bow of the *Guinevere,* his silver hair slicked to his head, his tanned body as sharp as a bronze blade against the sky. Rising up, held for a moment by sky wires . . . arcing down to slice the water . . . coming up once to hold an invisible offering into the air . . . then going down, down, down into a cold, dark world where he'd never have to remember what happened to Matthew or that Kim wouldn't marry him. Even though the rescue people brought Michael up a few hours after I called 911, I still thought of him in the Deep, cradled safely in the white arms of those ancient trees.

My sister turned to me. Her eyes were watery; her mascara was smeary. She didn't look much like a famous model. She leaned her cheek against mine. "I still loved him in a way, Sare-Bear," she said. Her voice was small and wavery. "Even at the end, when he thought I didn't."

I patted her curly, peach-colored hair as if it were me who was the big sister now. I went on patting and patting. After that, we didn't say anything more. We just hung on to each other till we landed in Indianapolis.

The service was held at the church where Michael had gone since he was a little kid. The same place where his brother Matthew had been buried from.

I was sure Michael's parents would be ogres or horrible people, like some parents you read about in books or see on TV. The kind who are stiff and cold and only want to be friends with other rich people and don't understand their kids. After all, Michael said they kept Matthew's pictures up all over the house and left Matthew's room as if he'd come back any minute.

But they were as ordinary as Mom and Dad, even though Dr. Miller was the kind of surgeon who opened people's chests and sewed up holes in their hearts or put in new valves or whatever needed fixing. They weren't much older than Mom and Dad, but of course when one realized they'd lost both their sons it made them seem awfully special. Fragile, as if they might break any minute.

My mother, that famous spaghetti maker, acted as if she actually were an old-fashioned Italian mama. She folded Mrs. Miller into her arms and they cried together as if they'd known each other a lifetime.

My dad, a man whose life had gone to the dogs and who didn't even own a suit (he had to borrow one from Uncle Ralph for the funeral), took Dr. Miller's elbow in that special way he has of handling animals and people. He steered him over to where they could lean against the wall next to a doorway going into the chapel. They talked quietly, not actually looking at each other, the way grown-up men sometimes don't.

That left Kim and Joey and me to huddle together on a bench in the foyer. "It's sort of scary," Joey whispered. "A funeral, I mean. Because it doesn't seem like Michael's really gone." His chin started to quiver so I put my arm around him. I knew it was exactly what Michael would've done himself if he'd been with us.

In a little while Michael's parents came toward us, smiling the wan smiles of people who are just getting over a long and terrible sickness. There were more hugs all around—Mrs. Miller had a smooth helmet of silver hair just like Michael's—then it was time for everyone to go into the chapel for the service.

We were the kind of family that didn't go to church as often as other people. We went mostly on big holidays like Thanksgiving and Christmas and Easter, but it felt kind of soothing to sit there with everyone who'd known the Millers forever, to see how the light filtered through the colored windows, to be bathed in sad music and smell the flowers that were clustered in banks of yellow and pink and white around the bier.

When the minister stood up behind a lectern of dark

wood with carvings of roses and vines on it, I wondered what he could say that would mean anything to everyone who'd come to listen.

"The pains suffered by the human body caused by illness and disease can be many," he began. "But the sorrows of the human heart often are beyond the wisest of us to understand."

That's when I knew other people understood that Michael's accident wasn't really an accident.

"Our mutual tragedy is that a person who endures sorrows of the heart, as did Michael Jeffrey Miller, often cannot explain his anguish to those he loves the most." To me, it sounded like the minister knew just the way it'd been.

"In turn, we who love such people—those people in our lives that are troubled by despair they cannot name—feel burdened by guilt and wish we could have helped them more." That's how Kim felt. I did too, even though I wasn't the person Michael bought a promise ring for.

When Michael talked about the stars, was he trying to tell me something more important? Should I have hugged him then, like Joey hugged him the day when Michael jousted with the stray?

"Michael was loved by all who knew him," the minister said. He was a tall man, thin and scholarly looking. "But sometimes the love of others isn't the only thing that's needed to get us through this earthly life with its unexpected griefs and woes."

The back of the pew was solid and friendly against my back. Beside me, Joey leaned into my shoulder and I rested my hand on his knee so he'd feel anchored too.

"You see, we must learn to love ourselves as well," the minister went on. "Just as importantly, we need to forgive ourselves for our mortal failings. We must seek forgiveness not only from a kind and loving God but from our own judgmental hearts."

Michael couldn't forgive himself. He'd been his own celestial judge and jury, just like I tried to be with Kim. Michael was right when he told me it wasn't Dylan Irving who came between him and Kim. It was his own judgmental self that did.

The smell of the flowers floated over me. At the beginning of summer, love in the Connelly family had been so simple. My parents loved each other and they loved us kids. Kim was bringing someone home for the summer that she said she loved. I hadn't liked him in the beginning, then I started to love him too. I loved a dog named Bingo. It didn't seem complicated at all.

But maybe love is really like those little Russian puzzle boxes that fit inside one another, each one a little smaller than the one before, till finally the last box is so tiny you can hardly pick it up except with tweezers. I mean, it's not like what it looks like on the outside.

"Today, we're gathered here together to say a loving farewell to the beloved son of Dr. and Mrs. William Miller. Let us bow our heads as we celebrate his life, and let us pray for the peace of his spirit in death."

Joey sniffled; Kim wept; Mom and Dad dabbed at their eyes. Mine stayed dry. I'd cried when the grief counselors talked to us about Eddie Ripley's brother, but now I couldn't.

After the service everyone went to the cemetery. Michael was laid to rest beside his brother on a high spot of ground under the blue Indiana sky, with lots of smooth grass and white headstones stretching in all directions. Far away was a dark line of pine trees that made me think of the ones on the far side of Echo Lake.

It was a pretty day, one of those warm, late summer

days when everything's suspended between the end of one season and the beginning of another. A day when you know things are changing, but you crave to hold on to what's been. Joey and I stood together, and he stuck his hand in mine. I was glad when sweat glued our fingers together.

We went home the next day, though the Millers asked us to stay longer. "We'd love to have you," they said in soft, tired voices.

"Running a boarding kennel is a lot like being a dairy farmer," Dad explained with his crooked smile. "Cows won't let you take days off and neither will a shedful of dogs." So we parted, and they said in a week or two they'd send someone to Brookfield to drive Michael's little green car back to Indiana.

The first thing I did when we got home was go out to check on Bingo. I spoke to each dog on either side of the aisle as I headed toward his run. When I got to Bingo's, I called out, "Yo, Bingo Yingo Zingo!", and he pressed hard against his gate, as eager to see me as I was to see him.

I wondered if Bingo remembered what he'd done, trying so desperately to find Michael, so I asked Dad if I could take him out and walk along the lake.

"Sure," he agreed. Then he gave me a steady, special look. Not sorrowful, but filled with something hard to describe. Regret, I guess, about how the summer had turned out. "Do you want me to come with you, Sarah?" he asked gently.

I was really glad he asked, because it gave me a chance to explain that I needed to be alone for a while. Alone except for Bingo, that is.

"How about next time?" I said, which saved me from actually saying no. He nodded. There were lots of things you didn't need to explain to my dad. He just seemed to understand the tough stuff.

At the edge of Echo Lake, Bingo sat at my left side, straight up with no lazy slopping over onto his butt, his head erect and ears lifted slightly. I felt him quiver, and held my breath, wondering if it was fear that made him tremble. I had my old sneakers on so I walked into the lake. He followed me as if he'd been doing it a lifetime. He looked up, his red tongue lolling out of his mouth. Right then, I'd swear that Bingo smiled at me.

"I love you, Bingo," I said, though I knew I wasn't supposed to love a dog that didn't belong to me. I glanced over my shoulder to stare at the place I'd last seen Michael Jeffrey Miller. The water was smooth and tranquil; there wasn't a cloud in the sky. Some tears came then. Not big ones. Just a few soft ones that rolled down and plopped onto my T-shirt and left dark spots like raindrops.

Then I remembered what the minister said. *We have to forgive ourselves too.* We have to keep on loving ourselves, no matter what. I wiped my nose against my knuckles and turned back to the kennel shed.

I put Bingo away after giving him a good workout in the arena, and when I went in the house the phone was ringing. Mom answered it, then held it out to me. It was Camilla.

"You said you'd take Abigail if we had to move," she reminded me. There wasn't any stress in her voice, as if she'd learned to live with what had to be. Camilla, who cried in gym class and on the bus, had finally learned how to accept what Michael never could: Once something's happened, you can't make it unhappen.

"We begged the apartment manager to let us keep her," Camilla explained, "but he said if he made an exception for Abigail pretty soon the place would be full of dogs and cats and canaries and who knows what else." She definitely was her old, practical self again.

I covered the mouthpiece. "It's Camilla, Mom. Can I take Abigail?" My mother nodded yes without saying, "Now, Sarah," or telling me we'd have to discuss it first.

"I'll come in with Mom tomorrow and pick her up," I told Camilla. "I'll take good care of her—and if you guys ever get a house again you can have her back, okay?"

Then I went out to the screen porch on the front side of the house. It would be sort of neat to have a cat. Maybe Abigail could sleep with me. I'd get her some special toys. A mouse that squeaked and a scratching post, to help her feel at home.

I thought about Emily, who told me her life wasn't over just because she'd had a baby. Camilla, who accepted that her folks wouldn't ever get back together. Dad, who said it wasn't the end of the world that we might not be able to go to that show in Milwaukee. Joey, who said it was no big deal he couldn't see Skippy Simpson all summer. Bingo, who'd dived over the side of *Guinevere* as if he'd been diving into water all his life.

Oh, Michael! Why couldn't it have been that way for you too?

I sat and rocked awhile, my mind sort of empty the way it can be after something huge has happened. Then I saw someone on a green bike pedaling up the road. Not pedaling fast, just taking his time, as if he had lots to spare. He turned at the mailbox.

I walked down the drive to meet Jason Conrad. I decided I'd ask him if he'd like to help me sand off the old name on our sailboat and paint a new one on. I'd found some paint in the basement, about the same color as the blue bottle on the kitchen windowsill that Mom kept filled with yellow strawflowers. I wanted to call her the *Gwenhwyfar* now.

A friend of mine who knew a lot about the days of King Arthur said that's a Welsh name, I'd tell Jason. *It means "white phantom."*

Jason knew a lot of stuff about a lot of different things besides health science. Maybe he even knew something about King Arthur and those faraway times. I might even tell him the story about Loon Woman, who made a necklace out of the pieces of her brother's broken heart. Because even though I didn't know much about love yet, I wasn't ready to give up on it.

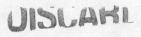